"I know the type of man I want,
Kate said confidently.

Just then, a loud crash reverberated through the building. Kate hurried down the stairway, her mouth dropping open at the whirlwind of dusty papier-mâché fragments blowing out of the downstairs office. She peered in nervously.

"What the hell is this?" A very tall, good-looking man was standing in the middle of the room holding a Cupid's arrow in one hand, as a thick layer of dust covered his obviously expensive suit. "What's going on here?" he said furiously.

Kate looked at him in horror, a myriad of emotions running through her mind as he stared dumbly at the arrow in his hand. Her lips suddenly began to twitch as a humorous thought struck her, and she couldn't refrain from grinning. "I think you just got hit by Cupid's arrow," she quipped. "You never know when he'll strike."

Dear Reader:

All of us here at Silhouette Books hope that you are having a wonderful summer, and enjoying all that the season has to offer. Whether you are vacationing, or spending the long, warm summer evenings at home, we wish you the best—and hope to bring you many happy hours of romance.

August finds our DIAMOND JUBILEE in full swing. This month features *Virgin Territory* by Suzanne Carey, a delightful story about a heroine who laments being what she considers "the last virgin in Chicago." Her handsome hero feels he's a man with a mission—to protect her virtue *and* his beloved bachelorhood at the same time. Then, in September, we have an extraspecial surprise—*two* DIAMOND JUBILEE titles by two of your favorite authors: Annette Broadrick with *Married?!* and Dixie Browning with *The Homing Instinct*.

The DIAMOND JUBILEE—Silhouette Romance's tenth anniversary celebration—is our way of saying thanks to you, our readers. To symbolize the timelessness of love, as well as the modern gift of the tenth anniversary, we're presenting readers with a DIAMOND JUBILEE Silhouette Romance each month, penned by one of your favorite Silhouette Romance authors.

And that's not all! This month don't miss Diana Palmer's fortieth story for Silhouette—*Connal*. He's a LONG, TALL TEXAN out to lasso your heart! In addition, back by popular demand, are Books 4, 5 and 6 of DIANA PALMER DUETS—some of Diana Palmer's earlier published work which has been unavailable for years.

During our tenth anniversary, the spirit of celebration is with us year-round. And that's all due to you, our readers. With the support you've given us, you can look forward to many more years of heartwarming, poignant love stories.

I hope you'll enjoy this book and all of the stories to come. Come home to romance—Silhouette Romance—for always!

Sincerely,

Tara Hughes Gavin
Senior Editor

KRISTINA LOGAN

Promise of Marriage

Silhouette **Romance**

Published by Silhouette Books New York

America's Publisher of Contemporary Romance

To my family
for their love and encouragement

SILHOUETTE BOOKS
300 E. 42nd St., New York, N.Y. 10017

ISBN: 0-373-08738-1

First Silhouette Books printing August 1990

Printed in the U.S.A.

KRISTINA LOGAN

is a former public-relations professional who spent several exciting years working with a variety of companies ranging from wedding consulting, to professional tennis, high technology and the film industry. Now the mother of two small children, she divides her time between her family and her first love, writing. A native Californian, she has lived all over the state and currently resides in Burlingame.

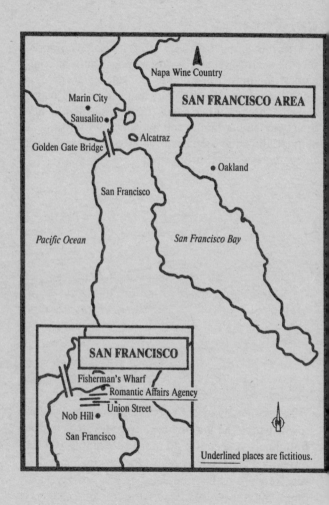

Napa Wine Country

SAN FRANCISCO AREA

Marin City

Sausalito

Alcatraz

Golden Gate Bridge

Oakland

San Francisco

Pacific Ocean

San Francisco Bay

SAN FRANCISCO

Fisherman's Wharf

Romantic Affairs Agency

Union Street

Nob Hill

San Francisco

Underlined places are fictitious.

Chapter One

Thirty-five minutes and twenty seconds, Kate noted with a sigh, as the bus turned onto Union Street. Commuting time was one factor she hadn't considered when she had opened her wedding-consulting business in the Marina district. At the time she had been looking for a romantic atmosphere and a reasonable price. She had found both in the old-fashioned Victorian house located on one of San Francisco's more popular shopping streets.

Unfortunately most of her business took her downtown, where the major hotels were located, and she found herself spending an inordinate amount of time traveling on buses or searching for parking places. But she couldn't really complain. It was exhausting at times, but it was also invigorating, because she was in business for herself. The creativity, the success was in her own hands, and that was a wonderful feeling.

The bus came to a jerky stop just a block away from the Romantic Affairs Wedding Agency, and she hastily pushed a pile of notes and brochures back into her briefcase as she prepared to get off. Stepping out into the warm afternoon sunshine, she took a deep breath of fresh air and started walking toward her office building, mentally preparing herself for the next meeting.

She smiled a hurried greeting at Mr. Ramoni, the local flower vendor, as she walked around his cart, which was parked at the bottom of the stairs leading up to her office. He had been selling flowers on their corner for the past twenty years and was one of the interesting characters who made Union Street so appealing.

She silently groaned as he motioned for her to stop. She had a tendency to run late, and getting caught up in conversations like this was the main reason. But she couldn't resist his friendly smile.

"Hello, Miss Marlowe," he said gruffly. "This is for you."

Her blue eyes opened wide as he handed her a perfect, long-stemmed white rose, her favorite flower. "Thank you," she replied, her voice mirroring her surprised expression.

"I tried your remedy," he said with an awkward smile, his weather-beaten face wrinkling with pleasure.

Understanding flashed through her eyes as he rocked back and forth in his old hiking boots. His rough appearance made a striking contrast to the delicate flowers that surrounded him.

"Did it work?"

He nodded his head up and down, an embarrassed twinkle coming into his dark eyes. "My Elena, she said she never had such a wonderful night. We felt like kids again."

"I'm so glad. You and Elena are a very special couple."

"We owe it all to you. If there's ever anything I can do for you, just let me know."

"Just be happy," she tossed out, waving goodbye as he went to help another customer.

She tripped up the steps to her building with a lighthearted smile. It was good to see Mr. Ramoni happy again. Her smile suddenly faded as she heard the grandfather clock chime five times. With a resigned sigh she jogged up the steep flight of stairs to her office and threw open the door with a breathless, apologetic smile.

"I know I'm late, but it wasn't my fault," she said immediately, taking in the empty office in one swift glance.

Liz Jamison calmly raised one eyebrow as Kate tossed her coat onto the antique coatrack.

"What happened this time—traffic jam, flood or an act of God?"

"A broken-down bus and a double-parked ice-cream truck," Kate replied. "Is Melanie here yet?"

"No, you're lucky. She isn't coming. Her bridal fitting got postponed until four, and she has a cocktail party to go to tonight. She's going to call and reschedule tomorrow."

Kate rolled her eyes and sat down in the chair in front of the reception desk. "I'm not surprised. This is the third meeting she's cancelled."

"I know. I told her we really have to meet soon if she wants to have a successful engagement party. It's only six weeks away."

"That's certainly not much time for what she wants," Kate replied, pulling the silver clip out of her black hair and letting the tangled waves tumble freely around her shoulders. She sat back in her chair, twirling the rose idly between her fingers.

"Who gave you the rose, a secret admirer?" Liz teased playfully, grinning at the darkening blush on Kate's normally rosy cheeks.

"No," she replied with a laugh. "It was Mr. Ramoni, and it's sort of a thank-you. He was really depressed last week about his marriage, and I gave him some advice."

Liz shook her head in mock disgust. "Don't tell me, it was another one of your romantic remedies."

Kate frowned at her sarcastic tone. "Well it worked."

"What did you prescribe this time, Dr. Marlowe?"

"Now why would you want to know that? You don't believe they work."

"Come on, tell me."

Kate leaned forward with a mischievous grin, her blue eyes sparkling brightly as she replied. "I told him to fill his bathtub with bubble bath, light a scented candle and pour two glasses of champagne into the nicest crystal he had. I left the rest up to him."

Liz burst out laughing. "I don't think I can picture that gruff old man and Mrs. Ramoni in the bath together. I can't believe they would fit."

Kate chuckled in return. "Well, apparently it worked. Maybe you should try it some time." She paused as Liz made a face that expressed her cynicism better than any words could. "Any messages?"

"They're on your desk," Liz answered. "Nothing urgent. How did your meeting with Davina Smythe go?"

"Don't ask. Davina's latest request is an ice carving in the shape of a thoroughbred racehorse, because her fiancé loves racehorses."

"What did you tell her?"

"That we'll do our best."

"Good luck."

"I want to make her happy," Kate said defensively. "This is her special day. I just wish she'd settle on one thing. First it was two doves, then bells intertwined, then a bouquet of roses, now a racehorse. I aim to please, but sometimes—"

"That's why I leave the brides up to you. Speaking of problems, we got a notice today stating that the bottom floor will soon be occupied, and would we please move our wedding supplies out of the room."

"That's just great. Where on earth are we going to put ten life-size cupids until Julia's wedding, which is still over a month away?"

"I have no idea, and I still don't know why you ever let her talk you into getting those. They look ridiculous. I can't believe she wants to decorate her wedding hall with them."

"I'll admit it's a little corny, even for me," Kate remarked. "But what I originally had in mind were a few six-inch statuettes to decorate the tables. I had no idea the ad was misprinted and six inches was really six feet. I was all set to ship them back when Julia saw them and thought they would be perfect."

"Maybe she'd like to keep them at her house," Liz suggested with a twinkle in her green eyes.

Kate grinned at the suggestion. "I seriously doubt it. I just hope we can find an out-of-the-way place to put them. Did the notice say who is going to be renting the office?"

"Nope. I guess we'll have to wait and see."

"It's a shame. I was getting used to having our own building and a little extra space to spread out in." She sighed and stretched her arms over her head as she got to her feet. "I guess I better go check my messages."

"Oh, one more thing before you go. Mrs. Hunt called with the directions to her party tonight, and I put them on your desk. She lives in the Sausalito Hills, but it doesn't sound too difficult to find. Apparently anybody who's anybody is going to be there tonight, so this could be a good opportunity for you to network. Our name is growing, but we could definitely use a few more high-society weddings."

"Right," Kate agreed. "Who knows? Maybe I'll meet an interesting man there."

"Good luck. I haven't found our clients' parties to be particularly good hunting ground."

Kate laughed dryly. "That's certainly true. Not that I have any intention of falling in love right now, I'm much too busy."

Liz smiled wisely. "Come off it Kate, you're a born romantic. You spend your days dreaming about Prince Charming. I'm just not sure you'll recognize him when you see him."

"I know just the type of man I want," Kate said confidently. "He'll be romantic—of course—"

"Of course," Liz echoed mockingly.

"Sensitive, caring—but not smothering, funny, cute, and he'll have a good sense of humor, a nice smile—"

"Stop already. I can't stand it. You're living in a dreamworld, my dear. There are no men in this city like that. In fact there are no men in this world like that."

Kate made a face at her sarcastic reply. It had taken Liz nearly three years to get over a very bitter divorce, and it was only in the last six months that she had begun dating again. It was not surprising that she was cynical about men. And Kate certainly had plenty of reasons to feel the same way. She had watched her mother go through a succession of men who never quite seemed to live up to her expectations.

"Are you leaving now?" she asked as Liz ran a comb through her short blond hair and reached into her purse for a lipstick.

Before she could reply, a loud crash reverberated through the building. They stared at each other in alarm, an agonizing thought occurring to Kate as the sound of swearing drifted up the stairway.

"You don't think—" she whispered as the phone rang.

Liz shook her head. "I think you better go find out. I'll get this."

Kate cleared her throat nervously, and with a resolute shrug of her shoulders she hurried down the stairway, her mouth dropping open at the whirlwind of dusty papier-mâché fragments blowing out of the downstairs office. She peered nervously into the darkened room, hitting the switch with one hand and gasping as light flooded the cloudy room.

"What the hell is this? And who the hell are you?" an angry voice demanded. A very tall, good-looking man was standing in the middle of the room, holding a cupid's arrow in one hand, as a two-inch layer of dust covered his obviously expensive suit. "What's going on here?" he said furiously, running one hand through his dark, curly hair, unaware that he had just streaked it with beige dust.

Kate looked at him in horror, a myriad of emotions running through her mind as he stared dumbly at the cupid's arrow in his hand. Suddenly her lips began to twitch as a humorous thought struck her, and she couldn't refrain from grinning as he stared stupidly at the remaining statues. "I think you just got hit by cupid's arrow," she quipped. "You never know when he'll strike."

He stared at her as if she were crazy, and she took an instinctive step backward as he put down the arrow and walked over to her. Wishing she could add a few more inches to her five-foot-three-inch frame, she squared her shoulders and tried not to look intimidated.

"What did you say?" he asked quietly, pausing just a few inches from her face.

She looked into his stormy face, her voice catching in her throat. "I'm sorry," she said finally, taking another step back.

He folded his arms in front of him, adding another streak of dust to his soiled white shirt, and studied her appraisingly.

She fidgeted under his gaze, but resisted the urge to look away. "You just looked so funny standing there." Her voice drifted away. "Can I help you clean up?"

"What you can do is tell me what the hell these—things—are doing in my office?" He waved one hand around the chaotic room.

Her mouth dropped open in surprise. "Your office? You're the new tenant?"

"I'm not only the new tenant, I'm also the owner." His voice was clipped and to the point as he began to brush the dust off his sleeves. His Ralph Lauren suit was completely ruined, she thought in dismay.

"I'm Kate Marlowe," she said finally, her earlier humor fading at his words. The last thing she wanted to do was offend the owner of her building. "I own the Romantic Affairs Wedding Agency upstairs, and these cupids are part of a wedding celebration."

He frowned at her explanation. "I wasn't aware that you had permission to use this office space."

Her blue eyes darkened at his arrogant tone. "Well, not officially, but since the room was empty, the building superintendent said he didn't think anyone would mind."

"He was wrong. And I expect this mess to be cleared out by nine o'clock tomorrow morning."

"Nine o'clock," she gasped. "We'll need a little more time than that. It's already past five now."

"That's your problem, Miss Marlowe. I have an interior decorator and a contractor meeting me here first thing Monday morning to prepare the office. I don't think I have to remind you that you are not paying rent for this space and are therefore not entitled to its use."

"But what am I going to do with all this?" she muttered under her breath, wincing at his derogatory glance.

"I think the garbage would be a good choice."

She flipped her hair back over her shoulder in irritation. "You don't need to be rude, Mr.—" She paused waiting for him to fill in his name, but he remained ominously silent. "I'll have these items removed by Monday." She spun around on one high heel and walked hastily out of the room.

The door slammed behind her, and she ran up the stairs to her office, a small smile curving her lips.

"What happened?" Liz demanded. "I was just about to come down and rescue you."

Kate shook her head, trying to stifle a chuckle. "Our new neighbor just had a run-in with our cupids, and I do mean run-in." She started to laugh in earnest. "You should have seen it. Here was this gorgeous man in a very expensive suit standing in the middle of a pile of rubble with cupid's arrow pointed right at his heart."

"I can't believe you're laughing. I thought I heard some nasty shouting down there."

Kate nodded, still grinning. "You did. He was furious. And by the way, we have to get them out by nine o'clock Monday morning."

"I don't think that's anything to laugh about. Rick and I are going to Lake Tahoe this weekend, and you're covering a wedding tomorrow. It's going to take some time to move all those statues. And where are we going to put them?" she asked, waving a hand around their tiny office. It was really just two rooms, a reception area and an office with a small storage room for all their materials.

Kate's grin faded. "I know it's a problem. I guess I'm just tired and a little slaphappy."

"Right," Liz said in disbelief. "So does this guy have a name?"

"I'm sure he does, but he didn't deign to tell me," she replied. "He was not at all amused by the situation. Apparently he has absolutely no sense of humor." She paused. "And I forgot to tell you the best part. He's not only our neighbor, he's also our landlord."

"But this building is owned by Fox Management. They have offices downtown in the Transamerica building."

"That's what I thought, but he said he was the owner."

"That's odd," Liz mused, getting to her feet. "Well, we'll have enough time to worry about that later. I think we better see about moving those statues. I want to go home, and you have a party to get to."

Kate nodded. "We can put them in here for now. I'll call around tomorrow and see if I can find an outside storage space." She followed Liz out the door. "I hope he's gone," she muttered as they walked down the steps. "I'm too tired for another lecture from Mr. Perfect."

Liz paused on the steps. "What did you say he looked like?" she asked curiously.

Kate rolled her eyes. "Tall, dark and handsome."

This time Liz laughed. "He does sound like Mr. Perfect."

"Don't you believe it. His looks may have been perfect, but his personality left a lot to be desired. He was arrogant, rude and completely insensitive. The less I see of him the better."

Chapter Two

Kate rolled her neck, trying to ease the tension out of her tired muscles as her tiny Honda crept along the Golden Gate Bridge. The heavy rush-hour traffic gave her plenty of time to review the day's events, and she couldn't help smiling. She knew she had a slightly wacky sense of humor; Liz was constantly pointing that out to her. But she thought even Liz would have cracked a smile at the sight of that elegant man holding a cupid's arrow in his hand.

She wondered idly what his business was. It had to be something serious for a man like that, high finance or stocks and bonds. She grinned. Of course he could be a mortician. That was serious, but he just didn't look the type. Whatever it was, he was definitely successful, that much she could tell by the cut of his clothes and the gold-and-diamond cuff links that had sparkled against his dusty attire.

She sighed at the thought of seeing him every day. The last thing she wanted was an unfriendly neighbor. Maybe she could patch things up in the morning, apologize for her behavior and start fresh. It was a pity he was so unfriendly. He was definitely the most attractive man she'd met in a long time.

Traffic sped up as she got to the end of the bridge, and it took only a few more minutes to reach the Sausalito exit. Stopping under the first streetlight, she took another look at the directions, although she had a fairly good idea of where she was going. Several of her clients lived in the posh neighborhood overlooking the San Francisco Bay.

The Hunts' house was just a few blocks off the main street, and she pulled up in front of the house with a broad smile. The parking valet curled his lips at her conservative Honda. The old blue car looked like an orphan next to the sparkling array of Mercedes and BMWs lining the street. Some day, she thought wistfully, ringing the bell.

The door was opened by a maid who took her coat and purse while a waitress offered her a glass of champagne. Very efficient, she thought, her experienced eye taking in the neatly attired help and their quiet, unobtrusive manner.

Taking a sip of champagne she glanced around, marveling at the spectacular view from the bay windows in the living room. She made her way slowly through the crowd, smiling politely as she tried to guess which of the elegantly dressed ladies was Mrs. Hunt.

That's when she saw him. She couldn't believe the coincidence, meeting the same man twice in one day. Of course he looked much happier now, and definitely more in his element. He was surrounded by a bevy of smiling women, some young, some old, but all beautiful and all rich, she surmised. He appeared rather disinterested in their conversation, however, his own gaze drifting lazily around the room. She turned around quickly, hoping to bury herself in the woodwork before he noticed her. The last thing she wanted was another confrontation, especially in front of a potential client.

Unfortunately her royal blue dress with its shimmering sequins stood out like a beacon in the darkness, and her flight was delayed by an overzealous waiter offering hot crab puffs. When the waiter finally moved away she was looking straight into a pair of mocking brown eyes. He had exchanged his dusty suit for an elegant black tuxedo, and she felt her heart skip a beat as he returned her bold appraisal.

She abruptly turned away, nearly knocking a glass of champagne out of another woman's hand.

"I'm sorry," she apologized quickly to the attractive blond woman in front of her. "I should have been more careful."

The older woman smiled easily. "There's no damage, dear. I wanted to introduce myself. I'm Olivia Hunt, and you must be Kate Marlowe."

Kate groaned inwardly. Wouldn't you know it would be her hostess?

"I'm glad you could come, Miss Marlowe. As you know, my daughter has just informed us of her plans to marry, and we are eager to do everything just right, starting with the engagement party and all the other social events right up to the wedding. I wanted you to come tonight so that you would have an idea of the type of parties we enjoy and, of course, have a chance to see the house and grounds in their best light."

"I understand," Kate replied. "And I must say that this party is excellent. You're obviously very good at planning your own parties."

Mrs. Hunt laughed softly. "That's true. I've been throwing parties for years, but to tell you the truth, I'm beginning to run out of ideas, and your agency came highly recommended. Danielle is our only daughter. We want something very special."

Kate smiled. "I think we can arrange an evening to remember," she replied sincerely. "But tell me, do you have anything special in mind?"

"Nothing in particular. But I do like creative and unusual ideas that are also tasteful. The engagement party will be a mix of Danielle's friends and mine, so we want to make sure everyone is happy. Tonight's gathering is somewhat representative of the group that will also be invited to the engagement party. Perhaps you could jot down a few ideas, and we'll be in touch later in the week. Now I really must go and see to my other guests. Please feel free to walk around and enjoy yourself.''

Kate nodded as her hostess moved on to the next group. Turning around she noticed that her landlord had disappeared. Just as well, she told herself firmly, it was time to get to work.

She spent the next hour going over the party details with a practiced eye and taking unobtrusive notes whenever possible. Mrs. Hunt was obviously quite a hostess. The buffet table was laid out with beautiful silver trays and a wide variety of gourmet delicacies. Even the birthday cake for her daughter was displayed atop a three-tiered silver platform, much as a wedding cake would be.

Rubbing her forehead tiredly, she wondered how much longer she should stay before making an exit. The smoke-filled room was beginning to irritate her sensitive eyes, and she decided to take a look at the gardens.

She made her way past the younger poolside crowd and headed down a garden path that led out to the edge of the hillside and offered a magnificent view of San Francisco and the Golden Gate Bridge. Delighted by the unexpected fairyland of lights, she leaned against the railing and drank in the view.

''Should I run for cover or did you come unarmed?'' a voice drawled mockingly from the shadows. Kate whirled around at the familiar tone. He was leaning indolently against the railing just a few feet away from her, his lips curved in a lazy smile.

"I thought that was you," she replied quietly, refusing to acknowledge the shiver that ran down the back of her spine. "Do you have a name, or shall I just keep making up names for you?"

His smile broadened into a grin. "I bet you've come up with some winners, too. My name is Barrett. Barrett Fox."

"The owner of Fox Management."

He tipped his head. "Kate, isn't it?"

"Yes. Kate Marlowe."

An awkward silence fell between them.

"I suppose I should apologize again for my statues," she offered halfheartedly.

"Ah, yes, the cupids. You know I've had some time to think, and I still don't understand what on earth you're planning to do with those ridiculous statues. Are they part of some strange wedding tradition, or just an exercise in bad taste?"

Her lips tightened at his harsh, teasing comment. "They're only ridiculous taken out of context," she defended. "If you could see them decorating the great hall of the Van der Kellen mansion, I'm sure you'd be impressed."

He laughed shortly. "I sincerely doubt that. I can't believe anyone would want to use anything so patently corny at their wedding. No, mark my words, that couple will be divorced within two years."

She stared at him in amazement. "Now why would you say that?"

"Easy. No man worth his salt would allow his bride to make a mockery of him. No, that poor guy will suddenly wake up and realize he's been taken for a fool."

"I think that's a disgusting thing to say," she said hotly. "You don't even know the couple in question, so I don't see how you can possibly make such a sweeping statement."

"I may not know them, but I've certainly met their friends," he said wryly, "and I have one ruined suit to prove it, not to mention what that statue may have done to my heart."

She blinked at his whimsical statement and sent him a wary look. "What do you mean, your heart?"

"I was referring to the legend of cupid and his deadly arrow."

"I don't think you have to worry. You look pretty hard-hearted to me."

A strange expression flashed through his dark eyes, but it was gone before she could respond.

"I certainly hope I am," he said cryptically. "Hard-hearted, I mean. Having a soft heart can get you into big trouble."

"I've often thought it was the other way around," she offered. "People without love seem so sad to me."

He shook his head in wonder. "Don't tell me, you're an old-fashioned romantic. I should have guessed. After all, you're a wedding consultant. I guess believing in love and hearts-and-flowers and—cupids is all part of your job.''

She frowned at the sarcastic edge in his voice, wondering what had happened to this man to make him so cynical.

"Anyway, it's my turn to apologize for yelling at you this afternoon. I had a very bad day, and I'm afraid your cupids were just the last straw."

She flushed guiltily at his remark. "I certainly would have removed the statues if I had known you were coming, but we didn't receive word until today, and I had just gotten in when I heard you swearing." She paused for a long moment. "I shouldn't have laughed at you. It wasn't very tactful."

"I've had a chance to calm down, and I guess I can see the humor in the situation," he said.

"You can?" Maybe he wasn't such an ogre, after all.

"Yes, I'm not normally so—"

"Rude," she put in, smiling at his wry expression.

"Rude," he conceded. "But like I said, I had a very bad day today, and I may have overreacted."

"I'm certainly glad to hear that, since we're going to be neighbors, and all. I'd like us to get along. Do you think we could be friends?" She extended her hand in friendship, not realizing what the warm touch would do to her pulse.

Barrett squeezed her slender hand gently, his eyes resting on the beautiful planes of her face. God, she was gorgeous, wild black hair and vivid blue eyes that lit up her face, a wide, generous mouth, and one of the sexiest smiles he had seen in a long time. Friends?

"Well, what do you say?" she whispered, shaken by the glittering of desire in his warm brown eyes.

He reached out and touched her lips with his fingers, tracing the gentle curve. "I think we could be a lot of things to each other, but I'm not sure friends is one of them," he said, his hand falling to his side.

Before she could speak he was gone, the scent of his after-shave lingering temptingly in the air. She turned and looked out over the view unseeingly, her heart pounding wildly in a mixture of relief and frustration. She touched her lips with her tongue, remembering his brief caress, the desire. He was right. They probably never would be friends.

It was late afternoon on Monday before Kate got into the office, having spent most of the day listening to musical groups destroy traditional wedding songs with their own creative touches.

The downstairs office door was closed when she went by, but the raucous sound of hammering and sawing confirmed the fact that Barrett Fox was indeed taking up residence. Fortunately he was nowhere in sight as she made her way through the common hallway. She wasn't quite ready to face him again.

Liz was on the phone as she entered the office and motioned for her to wait as she quickly finished a conversation with one of their vendors. Kate took a few minutes to sort through the music tapes she had collected, pushing the two promising ones aside for Liz to hear.

"What's up?" she asked, leafing through her briefcase for the accompanying song lists.

"You look terrible," Liz remarked.

"Thanks," she replied, closing her briefcase. "For your information, the Devlin Sisters play heavy metal, not Top Forty. My ears are still ringing. Do we have any aspirin?"

"Who would think a group called the Devlin Sisters would play heavy metal?" Liz asked in amazement. "They sounded harmless."

"Believe me, they weren't. Although they said they toned down for weddings. I can't imagine what their usual routine is. The little I saw included smashing a guitar over a drum set."

Liz laughed. "I thought you were going to start sending the brides out on their own to listen to bands." She dug through her drawer and tossed a bottle of aspirin to Kate.

"Thank goodness I didn't. Janine Hampton almost had heart failure when she saw the Devlin Sisters."

"How did the rest of your weekend go?"

"Okay. The Candleson wedding went fine, no problems, and I'm sure you noticed that the cupids are no longer in residence."

"You found outside storage?"

Kate nodded her head affirmatively. "They came and picked them up on Saturday afternoon."

"And how did the Hunts' party go?"

"Great," she said shortly. The last thing she wanted to talk about was the Hunts' party. It had left her feeling very unsettled.

"Is that it?" Liz asked curiously.

"Yep," she replied. She wished that was it. In fact she wished she could go back and do Friday all over again. There were a few things she would definitely change.

"Are you sure something didn't happen? You look sort of strange," Liz persisted. "You can tell me. Did you fall in the swimming pool or dump wine down your dress or get drunk and call Mrs. Hunt a—"

"Liz," Kate cried. "When have I ever done any of those things?"

"Well, let's see, you fell into the wading pool at the Jacksons' engagement party."

"I was pushed by their six-year-old twins."

"And you dumped wine, not down your dress, but down Mrs. Bradington's white gown at her elegant soiree."

"Her drunken husband grabbed the bottle out of my hand and he spilled the wine."

"And—"

"Stop already. The last thing I want to do is re-member every embarrassing incident that has hap-pened in the last three years. Besides none of those things happened at the Hunts' party."

"Then it must be a man," Liz said. "Am I right? You met someone, didn't you?"

Kate shook her head in disgust. "No. And there's nothing to tell. I spoke to Mrs. Hunt. I plan to write up a proposal for Danielle's engagement party. That's it, end of story."

"Wait. We do have one more problem," Liz said reluctantly.

"What?"

"Our new neighbor. He wants our pink-and-white wedding-bow wallpaper removed from the downstairs entry and stairwell."

Kate's mouth dropped open at the unexpected request. "That's ridiculous. We got permission from him or whoever runs his company to put up our wallpaper."

"He says that it's inappropriate for his business," Liz replied.

"Well, then he should just take his business back to wherever he had it before. I am not removing that wallpaper. It adds to the overall ambience," she complained, her temper flaring at his arrogant attitude. "In fact, I think I'll tell him that right now."

Liz grinned at the fiery light in her eyes. "Well, well, well," she remarked idly, as Kate literally flew out of the room. "That certainly got the blood pumping again."

Kate marched down the stairs and through the empty reception area. After a brief knock on his office door, she threw it open. At first she couldn't see much of anything through the dust from the saws and hammering. She walked over to one of the workmen and asked to see the owner. He simply pointed to one of the two inner offices. Holding her breath, she walked over to the half-open door and called hello.

Barrett Fox was in the midst of putting up a bookshelf, although at the moment he was studying a complex set of directions with an irritated frown. "I'll be right with you, Sandy," he said, without looking up.

Kate moved further into the office, the scent of her lilac perfume breaking into his reverie.

He sat back on his heels and sent her a curious look.

"Hello," she repeated crisply. She glanced around the room, trying to ignore the fact that dressed in casual jeans and sweater he was even more appealing.

"Did you want something?" he prodded impatiently. "Because as you can see I'm very busy."

Kate smiled at the pile of bolts and screws. "It doesn't look like you're making much progress," she said sweetly.

"What do you want?" he grumbled, staring blankly at the directions in his hand.

"I want to know just who you are and why you're here."

His frown deepened. "I told you my name. Barrett Fox."

"So you own Fox Management."

"Yes," he said abruptly, looking back at the directions in his hand.

She stared at him in disbelief. "You own a multi-million-dollar corporation that up until now had offices in the Transamerica Pyramid, and yet today you are kneeling on the floor of our tiny Victorian house trying to put a bookcase together. Don't you have someone to do that for you?"

"Of course I have someone to do this," he snapped, "but occasionally I like to do manual labor."

She laughed shortly. "Putting together a bookcase is hardly manual labor."

"Did you come here to irritate me?" he asked sarcastically, as she leaned over to take a look at the directions he was holding. He caught his breath as her silky white blouse opened just wide enough to reveal the soft swell of her breasts. Even dressed in a severely tailored black business suit, she was an incredibly sexy lady.

He dropped his eyes and tried to push the two pieces of hardware together with little success.

"I think you need to put this piece into this one," she said, oblivious to his wandering thoughts as she joined him on the floor. "Then take this bolt and hook the two together." She proceeded to do just that. "Perfect," she said triumphantly. "I hope I haven't dented your pride."

"Not at all," he replied with a glint in his eyes. "I'm perfectly capable of admitting that there are some things women are very good at."

The innuendo in his voice was not lost on Kate, and she instinctively jerked to her feet. "Well now that I've helped you, perhaps you can help me."

"So this wasn't a totally philanthropic gesture," he said cynically. "I should have known better."

"My partner, Liz Jamison, told me about your problem with the wallpaper. However, I would like to point out that we received permission to use that wallpaper from your company. Therefore I don't feel we should be asked to take it down."

"That was before I decided to take up residence here. And that wallpaper will definitely not help my business."

"What are you talking about?" she asked in exasperation. "How can wallpaper have an effect on a management company?"

He smiled at her bewildered expression. "Fox Management still has offices downtown," he explained. "These are my personal offices, to be used for my profession."

"I don't understand. What profession?"

His mouth curved into a wide smile. "I'm an attorney, Miss Marlowe, a divorce attorney."

"You're kidding."

"No. That's why I don't think wedding wallpaper is appropriate."

"But this is ridiculous. Why on earth would you want to move your offices right downstairs from a wedding-planning firm?"

"I didn't have any other choice," he said abruptly. "My downtown offices were recently destroyed by fire, and this is the only building we manage that has space available. So for the next six months to a year, this will be my new home."

She shook her head, muttering to herself. "I can't believe it—a divorce attorney? This is not going to work, at all. I certainly don't want my brides exposed to the senseless bickering of divorce clients."

His lips twisted in an ironic smile. "I feel the same way, only in reverse. No one wants to be reminded of his wedding day when he's getting a divorce. So I think the best thing we can do is to stay as separate as possible, and the common areas should be decorated in neutral colors."

"This is not going to work," she said more strongly.

"I think it will work out just fine," he mused, his dark brown eyes glittering with amusement. "We may both increase our business. You get them on the way in, and I'll get them on the way out."

She looked at him in disbelief. "You're disgusting!" she proclaimed, slamming the door behind her.

Chapter Three

W hat did he say?'' Liz asked, as Kate paced back and forth in front of her desk. "You look ready to kill someone."

"Not someone. Him," she said pointedly. "That man is the most obnoxious man I have ever met in my life."

"I guess he still wants the wallpaper removed."

Kate stopped in the middle of her pacing. "Do you know what he does for a living?" She didn't wait for an answer. "He is an attorney, but not just any kind of attorney. He is a bloodsucking, greedy, cynical divorce attorney."

Liz's eyes widened at her angry tone. "I can't believe it. I thought he was management or something."

Kate shook her head. "No, that's just a sideline. Breaking up marriages is his real profession."

Liz frowned at her description. "I don't think you can blame a divorce on the attorney."

"Maybe not," Kate conceded. "But I've never met an attorney who tried to help the couple work out their problems. They're too busy looking for a way to make more money."

"He really got under your skin."

"This is just crazy, Liz," she cried. "I hardly think a divorce attorney and a wedding consultant should be sharing the same office building."

"It is ironic."

"And we're going to have to put up with him for at least six months, maybe longer. Apparently his old offices were destroyed in a fire and they need extensive remodeling."

Liz nodded. "That explains it, then. This isn't really the neighborhood for a high-powered attorney." She got up from her desk and walked over to the coffee machine to pour them both a cup. "Drink this," she commanded. "And try to calm down. The Simses will be here in five minutes."

Kate took the cup with a grateful smile, acknowledging her point. "You're right. I guess there's nothing I can do right now. I'll just have to think of a way to get rid of Mr. Barrett Fox." A wicked gleam entered her eyes as she set her coffee cup down. "But it's business first, pleasure second."

* * *

"I'm really worried, Miss Marlowe," Jennifer whined. "I have to go down a very long flight of stairs in this incredibly full petticoat. I'm terrified I'm going to fall and disgrace myself."

Kate sent her a compassionate smile. Jennifer Aames was nineteen years old, the only daughter of a very wealthy industrialist. Her mother had died when she was fifteen and she was feeling extremely insecure about planning her wedding, even with Kate's help. Her latest crisis was the hoop-style petticoat that would be worn under her dress, billowing the material out at least three feet. Privately Kate thought the dress was very pretentious, but she had to admit that her ideas had been much different at nineteen than they were now at twenty-seven.

"It's very easy," she said patiently, as Jennifer tried to grapple with the hoopskirt over her tailored trousers. "You just put your hands on the front and pull it up slightly as you go down."

"But what do I do with the bouquet?" she wailed. "And I was thinking of carrying my mother's prayer book."

Kate wrinkled her nose as she thought for a moment.

"I just can't do it," Jennifer cried in despair.

"What if your father walks you down, instead of meeting you at the bottom?" Kate suggested. The only thing Mr. Aames had insisted on was that his daughter be married in his home, which unfortunately boasted a long and winding staircase.

Jennifer looked at her desperately. "There won't be room for both of us with this dress. I know I should have chosen something else."

"You can do it," Kate said. "Why don't you take that off, and I'll show you how to hold it."

Kate took off her suit coat so it would be easier to slide the hoop around her straight skirt. She put it on and groaned inwardly at the cumbersome feeling. No wonder Jennifer was worried.

"It's impossible, isn't it?"

Kate forced a smile on her face. "No. You just put your hands on either side and pull up. I do think we'll have to have your maid of honor waiting at the bottom to hand you your bouquet and prayer book, though."

Jennifer watched her walk back and forth with a more hopeful expression. "I can see how you do it in here, but there aren't any stairs."

Kate thought for a moment. "Well, that's easy enough. We can practice on the stairs outside. It's after five, and there won't be anyone around."

"Why don't you show me first, and then I'll try," Jennifer suggested.

Kate nodded and pushed herself through the office door. Thankfully Liz had already gone home for the day. She knew her partner would think she was absolutely crazy parading around in a hoopskirt. But she had always made it a point to give her clients as much service as possible, and if that meant showing a nervous bride how to go down the stairs in a hoopskirt, then so be it.

"You wait at the bottom, so you can watch me," Kate said as Jennifer walked lightly down the stairs. The twenty steps suddenly looked steep and intimidating, and she felt a little nervous as the wide skirt brushed against the wall on one side and the railing on the other.

"I'm ready," Jennifer called.

Kate took a deep breath and gathered up as much material as she possibly could and started her descent. She let her breath out as she made it halfway down without any problems. "See, it's not so bad," she called out, taking another few steps less cautiously. She was almost to the bottom when Barrett's door flew open unexpectedly. She took one look at his incredulous face and tumbled down the last three stairs, landing in an undignified heap at his feet.

Jennifer screamed in horror at her speedy descent. Kate tried to struggle to her feet, but her legs were tangled in the mass of material. "Help me, Jennifer," she said irately as the girl stood speechless. She was trying to look anywhere but at Barrett and some gorgeous woman who was watching her in absolute disgust.

The sound of someone chuckling turned her embarrassment to anger, and she struggled to her feet as Barrett's chuckle escalated into a laugh.

"What's so funny?" she demanded furiously, trying to look as dignified as possible.

He was laughing so hard he couldn't answer, just pointed his hand at her hoopskirt petticoat.

"What on earth is going on?" the blond woman demanded. "Who is this woman? And what is she doing parading around in her underwear?"

"This is Kate Marlowe. She owns the wedding agency upstairs," he explained with a twinkle in his eyes. "This is one of my clients, Monica Harding."

Kate tipped her head politely as she squirmed out of the hoopskirt and tossed it at Jennifer who remained speechless.

"I'm sorry for the disruption. This is a petticoat for a wedding gown, and I was simply showing Jennifer the right way to go down the stairs," she explained. "We thought everyone had gone home."

"You mean the wrong way, don't you? Unless you want all your brides to come rolling down the stairs," Barrett pointed out with a wide grin.

She shot him a dirty look but refused to disgrace herself any further, especially in front of such an interested audience. His smile faded as she surreptitiously rubbed her wrist.

"You're not hurt, are you?"

"As if you care," she muttered under her breath.

"I do care," he tried to say seriously, but another chuckle escaped as he looked at her bedraggled appearance.

She sent him a scathing glare. "I'm sure you were on your way out, so I won't keep you."

"Do you do this often?" he asked with a wicked gleam in his eyes. "I'd like to be here for the more revealing lingerie demonstration."

Monica frowned at his remark. "I think we should get going, Barrett. We only have a few hours before my party, and I need to take care of a few things."

He looked down at his companion with a soothing smile. "Of course, Monica. Goodbye, Miss Marlowe."

"Goodbye. Come on Jennifer," Kate said briskly. "Let's go finish our meeting upstairs." She didn't wait for an answer, but hustled her client back up the stairs as quickly as possible. She shut the door to her office and leaned against it, her cheeks scarlet with embarrassment.

"I'm really sorry about that," Jennifer said. "It's my fault we were out there."

Kate shook her head. "Don't be. It was my idea to practice, and I had no idea he would still be there."

"He certainly is good-looking," Jennifer remarked idly. "Of course his friend was, too."

"Yes," she muttered, wondering just what kind of friendship the two shared. He had referred to her as his client, but she doubted it was platonic, judging by the possessive grip Monica Harding had on Barrett's arm.

"Sometimes I wish Bruce looked more like that," Jennifer added wistfully.

"What?"

"Like that man downstairs. He was so masculine, you know what I mean? His looks weren't perfect like a model or anything, but he just looked so good. I can't think of the word."

"Try sexy," Kate put in dryly.

Jennifer smiled. "Definitely sexy. Of course he was pretty rude to you, laughing about your fall. That wasn't very nice."

"No, it wasn't. And I'm sure your Bruce wouldn't have done that."

"No, he would have been the perfect gentlemen. I love him very much. I know that he's a good man and that he'll be a good husband. But sometimes I just wish he was a little bit more exciting. That's silly, isn't it?"

Kate shook her head. "No, I think every girl would like a man that's exciting, someone attractive and mysterious, charming and romantic." She paused. "But no one is exciting all the time, Jennifer. It's more important to have someone you love, someone who will stick by you during the bad times."

"I know. You can't have it all, I guess. I'm sure that man downstairs probably has some faults."

"I'm sure he does," Kate replied with a twisted smile.

"At least we found out one thing," Jennifer added glumly. "I'm never going to make it down the stairs in that dress."

"Nonsense," Kate said, putting Barrett out of her mind. "I was startled by the door opening, otherwise I would have been fine. As soon as I'm sure we're alone, we're going to go out there and try it again."

"Are you sure?"

"Yes. I don't want you to remember my inelegant fall when you're walking down the stairs on your wedding day."

She opened the door and walked out to the stairway, calling out hello. No one answered. She turned back to Jennifer with a relieved smile. "Everyone's gone. Let's try it again, and this time it's your turn."

Several hours later Kate was sitting in her apartment, soaking her hand in a bowl of ice and muttering swearwords under her breath as she looked at the pile of ribbons, lace and potpourri she was in the middle of turning into wedding favors. There were only twenty left to do, but with her hand swollen up like a grapefruit, she had no idea how she was going to complete the job by morning.

Liz was out with her boyfriend, Rick, and according to her roommate wouldn't be back until late that evening. She had called everyone else she knew, but no one was available to help. She would just have to tell Kimberly that the bridal favors would be a day or two late. It wouldn't be a catastrophe. The wedding was still three weeks away.

She grimaced as she tried to stretch out her swollen fingers and with a groan she plunged her hand back into the ice just as the doorbell rang. Hoping it was Liz, she hurriedly wrapped a towel around her hand and opened the front door.

But it wasn't Liz, it was Barrett, and he was studying her faded blue jeans and sweatshirt with a familiar and amused smile. Damn him, he always seemed to catch her at a disadvantage, she thought, shaking her head as she noticed his sharply pressed gray suit and pristine white silk shirt.

"What do you want?"

"I came to see if you were all right," he said, pulling her hand out from behind her back. "And I can see that you're not."

"It's a little swollen, that's all."

"It could be broken," he said sharply, taking a look at her swollen fingers. "You should have someone take a look at it."

"I'm soaking it in ice," she replied, avoiding his penetrating gaze. "I'm sure it will be fine in the morning."

He sent her a long, serious look. "Can I come in?"

"It's late," she protested, feeling like a fool when he looked at his watch.

"It's only eight o'clock. I won't stay more than a few minutes."

She hesitated and then stepped back. "All right, but I warn you that everything is in kind of a mess."

He entered her tiny apartment with a small smile that grew into a wide grin as he looked around the cluttered room. It looked more like a bridal workshop than a home. A wedding-favor assembly line completely covered the dining-room table, and she had boxes and boxes of dried flowers and ribbons stacked against one wall. On an old oak coffee table, lace-covered photo albums in all stages of production were spread out, their ribbons and fabric intertwining in a rainbow of colors.

"You really take your work home with you."

"How did you know where I live?"

"My records. I have your home address on the lease you signed with us."

"Oh, right." Since he obviously wasn't going to leave, she walked over and cleared a pile of material off a stiff antique chair. She didn't want him to get too comfortable. "You can sit here if you like."

He frowned as he watched her pick up the books with her one good hand, wincing as her other hand struck the side of the lamp.

"Let me do that," he said, taking the books out of her hand. He pushed her gently down into the chair she had emptied, and then set the books on the floor.

"I wanted to apologize for laughing at you this evening. I had no idea you were hurt."

She softened at his genuine sincerity. "It's okay. I'm sure it looked pretty funny, just like you and the cupids. Only I don't think you found that particularly humorous at the time."

"Don't remind me," he groaned. "That was not one of my better moments. Maybe we should start over, forget about everything that has happened."

The twinkle in his brown eyes was very appealing, but she wasn't sure she could trust him. They certainly hadn't gotten along very well up to this point. She watched him settle his long frame down on one empty edge of the sofa. There was an amused light in his eyes as he looked around the room, and she had the feeling that he didn't take her or her business very seriously.

"Barrett."

"Yes?"

"As I told you before, I would like to be at least civil with you. We're going to have to coexist for the next six months to a year, so we should find some compromise to our unusual situation," she said, trying to ignore the devilish gleam in his eyes. When had she ever thought this man didn't have a sense of humor? He seemed to find their entire situation very amusing.

"I think civil would be good," he replied with a small chuckle.

"What's so funny?" she demanded. "Do I look funny? Is there something sticking out of my teeth or—"

"No, you look terrific," he interrupted. "I like the jeans and bare feet, and I've always been a fan of the Bears," he added referring to her UC Berkeley sweatshirt. "It's just that you're picking and choosing your words so carefully, I feel like I'm in a courtroom."

"I just want to put things in terms that you understand," she said pointedly. "When I mentioned before that I wanted us to be friends, you had a rather strange reaction.''

''Oh, that's what all this double-talk is about.''

She turned her head, wishing she had never begun the conversation. What could she say now? That she had thought he was going to kiss her that night, that she had wanted him to? Definitely not.

''I just don't want you to get the wrong idea, to think that because I want to be friends, I want to become involved with you,'' she said finally.

''Why would I think that?''

''I don't know. I just want to make sure that you don't.'' Her voice drifted away as he smiled. She felt like an idiot. She got to her feet, anxious to be finished with the conversation. ''If you'll excuse me, I have to get to work.''

''What are you working on?''

''I'm making wedding favors,'' she replied, walking over to the dining-room table.

After a moment he walked over to join her, looking down at the massive amount of materials waiting to be assembled. ''You do these by hand?'' he asked incredulously.

She nodded as he picked up a lace packet filled with scented potpourri and tied with a red ribbon announcing the wedding couple and the date.

''They're pretty detailed,'' he remarked. ''Do you put those little flowers on, as well?''

''Yes, everything. They're not too hard once you get started. But I have to admit I don't usually do them all myself. We have a couple of high-school girls who help, but this is Spring Break and most of them are away. This particular bride is very anxious to get them done as soon as possible. I only have a few more to do.''

"They look incredibly intricate," he added, casting a pointed look at her injured hand. "I don't think you're going to be able to manage with your hand the way it is."

"Probably not," she agreed, "but I'm just going to have to try. They were supposed to be done by tomorrow, and my partner, Liz, is nowhere to be found."

"I'd like to help you, but I don't think I'd be very good at tying little ribbons around lace packets."

She was startled that he had even considered helping. The thought had never crossed her mind, not that it didn't have some merit. A little wedding magic might be good for his cynical attitude. "I could always teach you," she suggested with a twinkle in her eyes.

"I think I'll pass," he said with a grin. "Not that I wouldn't like to help you. What are these over here?" he asked, walking over to the coffee table.

"Wedding-photo albums. They're my specialty, although I'm in the process of teaching some of the girls how to make them. Leather albums are very expensive, running close to three hundred dollars, whereas these are beautiful, sentimental and romantic, and only cost fifty dollars."

"I guess women like that frilly stuff," he replied, taking a look around her room. It was decorated much like her personality, old-fashioned antiques and lace curtains. There were little pieces of memorabilia scattered everywhere, photographs from her childhood, whimsical statements embroidered and framed, comfortable cushions trimmed with ruffles. He looked around in amazement, his eyes settling on a glass cabinet in one corner of the room.

"And those?"

"My castles," she said simply.

He gazed at the sparkling display of tiny miniature castles. They were done in different colors, some shiny and smooth, others rough and worn like the work of a child on a sandy beach.

"They're very—"

"Fanciful," she supplied. "I know. Some people think they're silly, but I've been collecting them since I was a small child. There's something about a castle that I find very appealing."

"I think you're a dreamer, Miss Marlowe."

"Definitely. Although at the moment I have little time for dreams."

"I know what you mean," he muttered, staring at the display with an unreadable expression in his eyes.

She had been referring to the work spread out in her apartment, but it was obvious that his reference went much deeper than that. "Do you collect anything?"

"Baseball cards."

"Baseball cards," she echoed, watching his face light up like a small boy.

"Over five hundred," he said proudly. "And some of them are definite collector's items."

"How interesting," she said halfheartedly. And how terribly unromantic.

"I'll have to show them to you sometime," he added. "Or maybe you'd like to go to the baseball-card convention at the Oakland Coliseum next month. It's fantastic. People from all over the country come to trade their cards. You can get some great cards there. I'm still looking for a Ty Cobb."

She smiled at his boyish enthusiasm, wondering if men ever really grew up. Barrett Fox was a successful, prominent attorney with good looks, and lots of money, and here he was raving about a baseball-card convention in Oakland. What a strange man he was.

"That's great. I like collecting things. It's like a link to the past." She sighed as her eyes drifted over to the stack of favors. "I'd better get back to work."

"I'll help you," he said suddenly, catching her by surprise.

"What?"

"The favors. You said you had a few more to do. You're not going to make it with that swollen hand."

Stunned didn't begin to describe the way she felt. "You're going to sit here and tie ribbons around my lace potpourri?"

"Is that what I have to do?"

She nodded. "Still interested?"

He looked down at his watch. Eight o'clock. Monica's party would be going on for hours. "Why not? I like new experiences."

"I wouldn't have guessed that about you," she muttered without thought.

"Good. I think predictable people are boring," he said, shrugging his shoulders out of his coat. "Let's get started." Barrett pulled out a chair and sat down. "What do I do first?"

"You fill the lace packet with potpourri," she said, trying to concentrate on the favors. She took a seat across from him and with one hand tried to show him how to put the favor together. It took him a few fumbling moments to get the flowers tied in with the ribbon, but she had to admit his first effort didn't look too bad.

Once he got started, he worked quietly and efficiently. Kate didn't speak, either. She was too bemused by his presence, too caught up in the warm, spicy scent of his after-shave, the tiny, dark hairs that curled enticingly around the silk of his shirt. He was a man of contradictions; cool and sophisticated, then friendly and warm. Unpredictable. He liked that. So did she.

Barrett had been working for nearly thirty minutes when the favor he was putting together suddenly fell apart in his hands, the lace and ribbons falling to the floor.

Instinctively they both reached for the favor at the same time, but as Kate grasped the lace, Barrett took her hand. His warm touch sent her emotions spinning. She looked at him and her heart seemed to stop. Slowly they straightened, their eyes locked in a gaze of unmistakable attraction.

Barrett pulled her hand to his lips, never taking his eyes off her face. He kissed her palm, and his tongue moved gently over her fingers, leaving her hot with desire. She felt herself drifting toward him, closer and closer until their faces were inches apart. She could see the faint shadow of his beard, the tiny laugh lines around his eyes. She noted every detail in that split second before his lips touched hers.

It was only a second before he jerked away, the loud squealing of her cuckoo clock effectively dousing the fire building between them.

"What is that?" he demanded.

"My clock," she said faintly, straightening up in her chair.

"Only you would have a damn cuckoo clock," he said with annoyance. "A totally impractical clock, not to mention loud and obnoxious."

"It has charm," she defended. "And it keeps very good time."

"Maybe so, but it has a lousy sense of timing," he remarked regretfully, staring into her lovely blue eyes. He thought for a long moment, debating his actions. Finally he shrugged his shoulders and got to his feet. "I should go. There are only a few more to do."

She nodded, trying not to look as unsettled as she felt. "Thanks for helping."

"No problem. Is there anything else I can get for your hand, aspirin or something?"

She looked down at her swollen fingers. She had been so caught up in Barrett that she had completely forgotten about her hand.

"No, thanks. I'll be fine. You've already done more than enough."

He smiled at her words and then put on his suit coat.

"Are you going somewhere special?" she asked wistfully.

"A party. I'm not very excited about it."

"Then why go?"

"Business. The woman throwing the party is a client of mine, and I promised her I'd attend."

"A divorcée? It doesn't sound like she's very unhappy about her divorce if she's throwing a party."

"She is and she isn't. Her husband left her for a younger woman, and she's trying to pretend that she doesn't care."

"That's terrible," Kate said. "Still, I can't imagine wanting to throw a party."

"I guess it's her way of coping."

"Maybe, but I certainly can't imagine wanting to throw a party in the middle of a divorce. It seems so cold, so heartless."

He nodded his head in agreement. "That's true, but people have to work out their problems in their own way. Monica is feeling rejected, undesirable, unloved. This party is her way of proving that she isn't any of those things.''

"Monica?" she asked, trying to ignore the dull ache that was growing in her stomach. "The woman you were with earlier, the gorgeous blonde?"

"Yes."

"She's very beautiful."

"Yes. But at the moment she doesn't feel that way."

"I see." She couldn't stop the sharp stabbing pain that entered her heart, but she could pretend that it wasn't there. "I guess you should go, then."

His lips tightened at her comment. "Do you have a problem?"

"Of course not. Your love life is your own concern."

"What makes you think Monica is part of my love life?"

"She's beautiful, available, lonely."

"What's your point?"

Kate flinched under his cold stare. She had no idea what her point was. She just knew that she didn't like the thought of Barrett and Monica being together. "I don't have one."

"What do you think, I'm some sort of a gigolo?"

"No, of course not. I didn't mean that, at all." Guilt flooded through her as she stared at the anger and pain in his dark brown eyes.

He nodded his head up and down without speaking, his expression a mixture of disappointment and anger. "I have to go. I hope your hand feels better in the morning."

She nodded as he walked out the door. Damn. What on earth had possessed her to snap at him like a jealous girlfriend? He had been so kind, so friendly. She walked over to the freezer and pulled out her bowl of ice, thrusting her hand into the frigid water. The ache radiated from her fingers all the way down to her heart.

Chapter Four

And then I toppled down the stairs, spraining my wrist in the process." Kate extended her swollen hand for Liz's inspection. It was much better this morning, only a few of the fingers were still puffy, and most of the movement had come back to her hand.

Liz looked down at Kate's hand in amazement and then back up at her. "I'll say one thing, Kate, you certainly lead an interesting life."

"I hardly think falling down the stairs qualifies as interesting," Kate retorted, picking up her coffee cup with her good hand.

"Yes, but doing it in a full hoopskirt under the eyes of a very attractive man is certainly innovative," she remarked, sitting back in her chair. "Now tell me what happened when Barrett came by your place last night.''

"I knew I shouldn't have told you that.''

"What happened?''

"Nothing. He apologized for laughing, said he was concerned about my hand. He was probably worried about a lawsuit or something.''

"I doubt that. Go on.''

"He saw what a bind I was in with the favors and he offered to help,'' she mumbled.

Liz's eyebrows shot up in surprise. "He helped you with the favors? He tied little ribbons around lace packets? I can't believe it.''

"I couldn't, either,'' Kate admitted. "But I was desperate. I couldn't find you. And Kimberly wanted them today.''

"I'm in shock. What did you do to that man?''

"Nothing. I think he felt guilty for laughing at me when I was hurt.''

Liz shook her head, tapping her pencil against the desk thoughtfully. "I think he likes you.''

"Don't be ridiculous,'' she snapped. "Even if he did, I'm sure he doesn't anymore. I wasn't very nice to him.''

"What do you mean?''

Kate sighed. "It's a long story.''

"Why don't you give him a chance,'' Liz suggested. "I like the sound of this guy.''

"Liz, he's a divorce attorney. I'm a wedding consultant. Don't you think there's a conflict of interest here?"

Liz smiled. "Opposites attract. It's happened before."

"That's true. But not this time." Kate picked up the stack of phone messages on the corner of Liz's desk. "I can't believe the number of calls we're getting. You must be going crazy answering the phones all day."

"No problem," Liz replied. "I'd rather talk to the brides on the phone than watch all that affectionate oohing and aahing when they come into the office."

Kate laughed. "They're not all that bad. We've been getting quite a few older brides these days, and they are definitely past the cooing stage." She set the stack of messages back down on the desk. "Business is certainly booming."

"And it's only April," Liz replied. "I also got two more calls this morning that aren't in there. One girl is getting married in two weeks and wants to know what we can do for five hundred hundred dollars."

"What did you tell her?"

"I told her we were booked up right now," she said decisively as Kate began to interrupt. "I know what you're going to say. You hate to turn anyone down, but even you can't put on a three-ring circus in two weeks, not for five hundred dollars, anyway."

"Maybe not a three-ring circus, but surely we can help her out." Kate argued, knowing that her partner was probably right. "I just can't believe that we're too successful to help people on a small budget. I don't want to become one of those snobby party givers with no time for the little people."

"Okay. I knew you were going to say that, so I got her name and telephone number," Liz said, handing her another slip.

Kate laughed. "Am I that transparent?"

"Only to me, kiddo. Everyone else thinks you're a sophisticated businesswoman," Liz replied as she got to her feet. "I know you prefer dealing with the average bride rather than those upper-crust socialites. But I'm here to make sure we make money, and that's where the money is."

"I know. I don't know where I'd be without you. And speaking of upper-crust socialites, I'd better call Davina and see if she has made any decision about her ice carving."

"Good idea. I'm going to be out most of the day. Gary is finally available to do the videotaping. I thought I'd take him around to a vendor in each category, a bakery, florist, hotel, restaurant, and show him the kind of shots we want. Then he can handle the rest of the appointments on his own. He'll have to do a lot of taping on the weekends, because I want to show the banquet rooms in their full glory, and they just don't look the same without all the wedding trimmings."

Kate's eyes lit up with pleasure. The videotape library was her brainchild. It was a way of visually showing a client all the different services that were out there, without actually taking her around to each place. They could sit down in a comfortable chair and leisurely review banquet rooms, photography samples, floral bouquets and cakes. The time saved would be substantial.

"Great. I'd really like to have at least a portion ready for the bridal show next month."

"Yes," Liz agreed. "We'll be the first wedding agency to have a really high-tech, professional presentation."

"But we're not going to lose the romance, either. I still plan to decorate the booth with lace-and-satin trimmings, and of course we'll serve chocolate truffles, as usual," she said. "I am a little concerned about the video being too boring. I think we need to jazz it up, not just show cakes and wedding bouquets but perhaps show how they're made from the very beginning. With the cakes we can go into the kitchens, show them being baked and decorated and later assembled. With the flowers, we can go to the Flower Mart and show how they select the flowers that go into the bouquets, maybe do a piece on what each flower means."

"Stop already. I can't keep up," Liz said laughingly, jotting down Kate's suggestions on the notepad. "Those are all good ideas. I'm sure Gary will be creative. He thinks like you do. What's your schedule for today?"

Kate grimaced. "Follow-up. I don't have any meetings until four, so I think I'll catch up on the paperwork."

True to her word, Kate spent the rest of the day returning phone calls and finalizing details. They had weddings scheduled for almost every weekend, and it was quite a feat to keep everything straight. In addition to the weddings she had a couple of engagement parties to coordinate, as well as bridesmaids' luncheons.

Just before four she threw down her pencil and stretched her arms over her head. She needed a short break before her next appointment, just so she could keep all the details straight in her mind. With a sigh she stood up and walked over to the window. Pushing it open, she let the cool, crisp air flow through her stuffy office.

The sound of laughter drifted through the air. Down below, Union Street was bustling with tourists and natives alike enjoying the warm, springtime weather. The street was filled with charming Victorian houses, tiny boutiques and open-air cafés that created a holiday atmosphere all year long.

Looking out at the sidewalk juggler, she thought again how lucky she was to be living and working in San Francisco. It was a far cry from her early childhood days in the sleepy town of Mendocino, but she was glad to be here and not there. The breathtaking beauty of her original home had never been able to make up for the loneliness in her early life.

She blinked twice, forcing the unwelcome thoughts out of her head. She was past all that now. The future ahead of her was bright and exciting, the kind of life she had dreamed about. That was what mattered. Nothing else. She turned away from the window as a sharp knock came at her door.

"I'd like to reserve the Museum of Modern Art for the reception," Courtney said firmly. "I want something different, avant-garde."

"It will certainly be that," Kate conceded, smiling politely at the young woman seated in front of her.

"Can you handle that?" Courtney asked doubtfully. "I'm very hesitant about turning over my wedding to a stranger, but my mother insists that we need professional help."

"I'm sure we can work out everything to your liking."

"Well, this is a rather small agency. I was expecting something much larger, not this quaint, little office." Courtney's lips curled with distaste. The lacy white doilies on the end tables and the dried flower arrangements filled with wedding favors were obviously not to her liking. "I'm really not one for fuss and frills," she said, tossing her elegantly coiffured head in distaste. "I want something very sophisticated."

"I'm sure we can coordinate everything to your satisfaction," Kate said soothingly, her lips tightening as Courtney tossed an engraved napkin down on the table.

"For instance, this type of napkin will not do. I don't want anything childish at my party."

Kate picked up the offending napkin and pushed it out of sight. This was the way things had been going all day. Every sample she brought out, Courtney tossed aside as being too corny, too childish, too romantic, too whatever reason she could think of.

"We are here to service you," Kate said. "We don't do anything you don't want us to do. I would like to point out that with a small agency like ours you are assured of a very personal approach. I don't think you'll be disappointed by our services."

"Very well, but I expect undivided attention. I'm willing to spend whatever amount of money it takes to ensure that I get everything I want."

Kate forced a smile onto her face. For two cents she'd tell Courtney to take her wedding somewhere else. But unfortunately they weren't talking about two cents, they were talking about a forty-thousand-dollar wedding, and Liz would kill her if she let Courtney go.

"Now, I'd like to discuss the ceremony," Courtney continued, stopping abruptly as the sound of loud voices rang through the building. "What on earth is that?"

"I don't know," Kate said apologetically. "Let me shut the door."

She walked over to the doorway just as a string of obscene swearwords floated up the stairway. Kate flushed as a man and a woman exchanged sexual insults that rang clearly through the building.

"What is going on? Is that another bridal couple?"

"I seriously doubt it. They probably belong to the office downstairs, which specializes in divorce law."

She closed the outer door and the inner door, but still the voices echoed through the old building. Unfortunately Liz had gone home for the day, so she couldn't go down and demand quiet. Where on earth was Barrett? Why didn't he try to stop their insane bickering?

Courtney tried to continue, but they were both distracted and finally Kate interrupted her. "Let me just tell those two to take their argument elsewhere."

She marched down the stairs, her annoyance turning to fury as Barrett stood listening to the man and woman vent their anger.

"What on earth is going on?" she demanded, stopping halfway down the stairs.

"They're having a minor disagreement," he shouted back, running one hand through his hair in agitation.

"Well, do something," she ordered.

He turned back to the arguing couple who were standing no more than six inches from each other but were yelling at the top of their lungs. "Gary—Janice," he called. "Please, calm down."

They both ignored him and he threw up his hands in disgust. "See what I mean?"

Kate took a deep breath, furious at the disruption. She stomped back up the stairs and into her office only to come face-to-face with Courtney, who was obviously on her way out.

Kate tried to apologize, but Courtney was not about to be placated. "This is totally unprofessional," she said angrily. "I'll expect my deposit back in the morning."

"Please, this is a very unusual occurrence," Kate said. "Why don't we meet tomorrow at your home. Then we can avoid any other unfortunate situations."

Courtney hesitated, still plainly irritated by the events. "All right. But you'll have to call me for an appointment. I don't have my date book with me, and I'm not sure I'm free tomorrow. This is really very inconvenient."

"I agree, and I'm sorry. I'll call you tomorrow," she said hastily as Courtney's ramrod-stiff back disappeared out the door. She was just grateful that Courtney hadn't walked out on their contract. Her wedding fee was going to be the backbone of their spring budget.

She shook her head as the argument downstairs suddenly escalated. Damn Barrett Fox. This was all his fault. He probably thought it was just an amusing problem. He was content to stand there and let those two shut down her business, but she certainly wasn't going to put up with it. Obviously talking at them, even yelling at them wasn't going to accomplish much. She could call the police, but that would probably take too long. A wicked glint came into her eyes as she spied the water pitcher standing on the corner table.

"This should do the trick," she said, picking up the pitcher. It was only a quarter full, but that should be enough to get someone's attention. She walked down the stairs and noticed that Barrett was nowhere in sight. The coward. He had probably gone home and left those two to destroy the building.

"Excuse me," she called out loudly.

"Stay out of this," the woman shouted, without missing a beat in her continuing tirade.

"Look, this has got to stop," Kate added. "This is a place of business." Neither one paid any attention to her, and Kate's irritation turned to full-blown fury when the woman grabbed the large brass coatrack at the bottom of the stairs and pushed it over, narrowly missing her opponent. Without further thought, Kate raised her arm and tossed the water into their faces.

Time stood still as two dripping faces looked at her bewilderedly, and the resulting silence was deafening. Kate eyed them warily, wondering if she had gone too far.

"Well, well, well," Barrett said, standing in his doorway. "Very nice."

"This is outrageous, Mr. Fox," the woman said, finally getting her voice back. "This is a five-hundred-dollar dress." She glanced down at the rumpled silk in complete dismay.

"No, your behavior is outrageous," Barrett replied angrily. "I will not tolerate this type of behavior in my offices. In fact I have just called the police, and they should be here at any moment to see that the two of you conduct your argument elsewhere."

The woman's mouth dropped open at his statement. "He's right, we should go," the man said,
looking first at Barrett's stony expression and then at
Kate's angry face. "I certainly don't want this to get
into the papers."

"You and your publicity, that's all you care about,"
the woman said angrily.

Kate sighed. It looked like the water was only a
temporary setback. They were ready to start the second round. But before they could say anything further, Barrett opened the front door and literally
pushed them both onto the doorstep, slamming the
door behind them, and turning the dead bolt with a
resounding click.

He turned around with a guarded expression on his
face, and Kate stared back at him uncertainly. She
didn't know what to expect. Thoughts of possible
eviction sprang to mind as she shifted back and forth
nervously, hoping he would speak first because she
couldn't think of a thing to say.

"I'm sorry about that," he said, leaning back
against the door with his arms crossed in front of him.

She let out a long, deep breath at his words, relief
spreading through her body as she realized he was
more embarrassed than angry.

"This was our first meeting and our last," he
added. "I had no idea they were going to get involved
in such a violent argument."

"They almost lost me a client," Kate said quietly.

His lips tightened at her pointed remark. "I hope the word 'almost' means you were able to smooth things over."

"Yes, but I can't understand why you just stood there," she complained, not willing to let him off the hook completely, no matter how much the soft plea in his eyes stirred her.

"Actually I had just come out of my office when you came down the stairs. I was on the phone and apparently their argument started before they ever got into the building. I've seen these types of things before. The bitterness in a divorce case can be brutal. And that woman just found out her husband's had a lover for the past five years who is now pregnant. Naturally she's a little upset."

"A little upset?" Kate echoed in disbelief. "If I were him, I wouldn't turn my back on her. She already tried to injure him with that antique coatrack."

"I agree," he said dryly. "Perhaps now you can understand my attitude about marriage. Those two were just one of many, many unhappy couples who go through a divorce every year."

"But you only see the unhappy people," Kate protested. "Every day I work with people who are madly in love, excited about their lives, really happy."

"That's before they get married," he said cynically. "Give 'em a couple of years."

She shook her head in frustration. "I just wish you would open up your eyes and see the other side of the coin."

"I have seen the other side of the coin. I was married for three years. And we started out just like everyone else, sappy about each other." Bitterness ripped through his voice.

"So, what happened?"

A host of emotions flashed through his eyes as he considered her question. Before he could answer, a knock came at the door. "That's probably the police. I called them when it appeared that the Bensons were completely out of control." He opened the door to two uniformed officers standing on the landing.

"We got a call about a disturbance," one officer said, taking a good look at Kate and then at Barrett. "Is there a problem here?"

"No, the problem just left," Barrett replied.

"Are you all right, miss?" the officer asked, directing his comment to Kate.

She looked at him in surprise. He thought she and Barrett were the ones who had been fighting. "I'm fine. The two people who were arguing just left."

The officers stared at them thoughtfully. "If you're sure," one said firmly.

"I'm the one who called you," Barrett said with annoyance.

"Okay, well let us know if you have any more problems," the officer replied as Barrett shut the door behind them.

Barrett shook his head. "What a day."

"You can say that again," she said, rubbing out the crick in her neck. "I thought I had it bad with the arrogant Courtney Brooks, but compared to your clients she's a delight.''

"Unfortunately people do not look their best during a divorce. And those scenes are a nasty part of the job.''

She started to turn around and then paused at the weary tone in his voice. "Then why do you do what you do?''

He shrugged. "Because people going through a divorce need help. They're too emotional to take a step back and divide up their property equally. They need an objective observer who can help them straighten out their problems." He paused. "Are you finished for the day?''

"Why?'' she asked warily.

"I'd like to take you out to dinner.''

She looked at him in surprise. The last thing she had expected was a dinner invitation. "Why?'' she asked again.

A lazy smile curved his lips. "Because it's been a long day for both of us, and I'm hungry. I thought you might be, too.''

"Well, yes.''

He folded his arms in front of his chest. "So what's the problem?''

She could think of about a hundred different problems, but she settled for the most basic one of all. "For one, we don't like each other very much.''

He laughed at her candid comment. "You certainly believe in telling it like it is.''

"I don't like to play games."

"Good, then I think we'll get along just fine. I don't like to play games, either. And the fact of the matter is that you intrigue me."

She twisted one strand of hair nervously, as his eyes glittered with desire. "Is that good or bad?"

"I'm not sure. Why don't we find out? Call a truce for the night. Besides you owe me one. I helped you make those ridiculous favors. The least you can do is keep me company while I eat."

He had a point, but remembering how poorly their previous evening had ended she wondered if it wouldn't be safer to keep her distance. She didn't trust Barrett Fox, still she had to admit he intrigued her, too. She should say no, she meant to say no, but when he looked at her with those intense brown eyes and that lazy smile the only thing she wanted to say was yes, and before she knew it she was comfortably ensconced in a silver-gray Mercedes.

Chapter Five

Within minutes Barrett pulled into the North Beach district, famous for its excellent Italian cuisine. Kate's mouth began to water at the sight of Italian Joe's and Mama Leone's, but when Barrett helped her out of the car he turned toward a long, dark alley, away from the more popular, well-known restaurants.

"Come with me," he said, taking her hand and tucking it under his arm. He led her down the alley and then into a stairwell. The only sign for the restaurant was a simple gold placard that said "Sonny's" on the door.

She blinked rapidly as they entered the darkened room, her eyes taking a moment to adjust to the candlelight. There were only about twenty tables, and most of them were already filled, but as soon as Bar-

rett gave his name the waiter led them to a cozy corner booth in the back of the room.

The booth was surrounded by glass panels on three
sides, affording them a tiny island of privacy. The soft
strains of opera playing lightly in the background
created a warm atmosphere that in Kate's mind was
quite romantic. She was surprised at Barrett's choice.
She thought something glitzy, more modern would be
his style.

After the waiter took their drink order, a very short,
round man standing about five and a half feet tall and
two feet wide, with a ridiculously curling moustache,
brought their menus over and greeted Barrett in effu-
sive Italian. Kate's eyes widened when Barrett responded in kind, and he turned to her with a grin.

"Don't be too impressed, my Italian is limited to a
few greetings, a couple of swearwords and—"

"The words of *amore*," Sonny finished for him.
"Who is this lovely lady?"

"This is Kate Marlowe," Barrett introduced. "My
good friend, Sonny Moretti."

Sonny took her hand and kissed it with a flourish.
"I am pleased to meet you, and for you and my good
friend I will make the finest dinner. You leave it up to
me, yes?"

Barrett looked expectantly at Kate and she nodded.
"I'm sure whatever you make will be wonderful."

"It will be," he promised. "It's been a long time
since you've come to visit me," he said to Barrett. "I

thought perhaps you had developed a taste for something finer."

Barrett shook his head. "There is nothing finer than your pasta."

Sonny beamed at his response. "For that I will also send over a bottle of my best wine."

Kate smiled to herself as Sonny gathered up their menus. Barrett certainly had a charming side to him.

"What's so amusing?" he asked, watching the candlelight play across her face. Her beautiful, thick hair was pulled back in a French braid with only a few wispy bangs dusting her forehead, and he felt his breath catch in his throat when she turned her sparkling blue eyes on him.

"You are," she replied. "You have a way with words—in any language."

"I'm a lawyer, words are my business." He frowned as her smile faded at the mention of his profession. "I'm really not that bad, you know. I help people salvage as much as they can out of their marriage."

"You mean money, possessions," she said flatly.

"Of course I mean money and possessions," he said in exasperation. "But that's not everything. There's also pride and self-respect and mutual understanding. Those things are important, too. Without laws, attorneys and judges, innocent people could get taken advantage of," he said passionately, resting his elbows on the table as he studied her skeptical expression.

"For instance, just yesterday I met with a woman who had been married for twenty-seven years to a very successful doctor. They married young and she spent the first five years of her marriage putting him through medical school. Then they had three children she raised almost single-handedly while he was pursuing his specialties and building his practice. After twenty-seven years of marriage, he walked out. It was over, just like that." He snapped his fingers for emphasis.

"I don't understand people like that," she remarked.

"Unfortunately it's not a unique story. It's happening more and more." He bent his head, his long brown lashes covering a fleeting expression of pain. She felt foolish and naive.

"I've never really looked at things that way before," she said thoughtfully. "I have a tendency to believe that people who get divorced just didn't work hard enough. So many people just give it a try on a whim and then when the going gets rough they bail out," she replied.

He nodded, pleased by her honesty. He paused as the waiter poured them each a glass of wine. "Perfectly true," he continued. "But everyone has to do what's best for them. Sometimes people don't have a choice." His eyes clouded over as he took a sip of his wine.

"What happened to you? Unless you'd rather not talk about it?"

"It was a long time ago," he said dismissively. "Caroline, my ex-wife, left me for another man. I probably should have seen it coming, I'm sure there were signs, but I was too busy." He paused, reflecting on the past. He had made so many mistakes.

"Busy getting your career going?" she prodded gently.

He looked at her with a wry smile. "There was that, yes," he admitted. "But there was also my sister, Sarah. Our parents died in a car accident when she was fourteen. We had no other relatives, so I became her legal guardian. She moved in and Caroline moved out."

"You're kidding? Your wife moved out because you wanted to take care of your sister?"

"I'm sure that wasn't her only reason," he said tightly, taking a long sip of his wine.

"She doesn't sound like a very nice person."

"Well, she wasn't a particularly nice person. Beautiful on the outside, but not on the inside. It was probably good that she left, though. Sarah had enough problems dealing with our parents' death. I didn't want her to go through anything else."

She fiddled with her fork as she thought about what he had said. Perhaps she had been too hasty in judging him. She looked up and started to speak, but the words caught in her throat as she saw Barrett watching her with a look of exquisite tenderness.

"You look very beautiful in the candlelight," he said deeply, his brown eyes caressing her face. "But then you look good in bright lights, as well. There's a certain quality about you that's very intriguing."

"You said that before," she said, trying to quell the uneasy fluttering in her stomach.

"I guess I just can't figure you out."

"I'm not very complicated."

He laughed softly. "All women are complicated. Every action is a contradiction. They say no when they mean yes. They say yes when they mean no. When you ask them what's wrong they say nothing, then break down in tears." He shook his head in frustration. "I freely admit that your sex is a complete mystery to me, especially you." He rested his elbows on the table as he looked into her eyes. "Are you an old-fashioned girl or a modern woman?"

"Why can't I be both?" she challenged.

His smile was a little too smug for her taste. "The two aren't very compatible."

"I don't know about that. I think a person can be many different things. Take yourself, for instance."

"I'm not sure I want to hear this," he protested, as the waiter brought over their salads.

She waited until they were alone again, reluctant to discuss anything so personal in front of a third party.

"It's not that bad," she said. "I was just going to say that you're an interesting mix, as well. When you're around me you're the cold-blooded cynic, making disparaging remarks about my romantic ideas. But then, on the other hand, you feel so deeply for your clients, like that woman you told me about, that I start thinking maybe you're not so bad after all."

"You mean you might even like me," he teased.

"I wouldn't go that far."

He refilled their wineglasses with a warm smile.

"Tell me about your life, Kate. Any skeletons in the closet, or are you as pure as you appear?"

Her rosy cheeks paled at his whimsical statement. She didn't want to talk about her past.

"Did I say something wrong?" he asked quietly.

"No, of course not," she said with a forced laugh.

"Are you going to answer my question? Are there any skeletons in your closet?"

"I'm not Pollyanna if that's what you mean," she said, refusing to meet his penetrating eyes. "I've had the usual social life, boyfriends and such, nothing particularly exciting."

"No one serious?"

"No."

"Why not? A romantic like you, I would have expected dozens of men."

"I'm very busy with my work," she explained.

His look was clearly disbelieving, but fortunately he let the matter drop and they spent the next few minutes concentrating on their salads.

"What about your childhood?" Barrett enquired after a moment. "Was it filled with the usual happy rituals of adolescence?"

"Happy enough."

"Did you grow up in San Francisco?"

She shook her head. "No, in Mendocino, about four hours north of here."

"Yes, I've driven through there. It's beautiful country. Why did you leave?"

"I wanted to start a business," she replied quietly, not wanting to admit that that had been only part of the reason. "And it was time to move on."

"Really?" he asked, his brown eyes studying her with an intensity that made her very uneasy. "Why are you so reluctant to talk about your past?"

"I'm not. There just isn't much to tell."

"I don't think so, Kate. I can see something in your beautiful blue eyes that tells me there's much more to your story than you're sharing. In my business I've learned to recognize a half-truth when I see it. Otherwise I'd be looking like a fool more often than not. There's always something in the background of someone's mind that he doesn't want to talk about."

"Well, maybe you should respect other people's privacy," she said with annoyance, as his comment hit home.

He stared at her in surprise. "Is that what you want me to do? Respect your privacy? Fine, that's no problem. I thought we were trying to get to know each other here, but obviously I was mistaken."

She sighed in complete and utter frustration. "Why do you always twist my words around?"

"Am I doing that?"

"Yes, you are. Maybe dinner was a mistake."

He put a hand on her arm as she started to rise. "Don't go, Kate. I'm sorry if I offended you." He shook his head regretfully. "I really would like to get to know you better, and I guess it bothers me that you don't feel the same way."

She looked at him, baffled by the hurt note in his voice. "I didn't say that. I would like to get to know you. Just don't push me so much. I feel like I'm on the witness stand."

"Sorry, I guess it comes with the territory."

"Do you think there's anything that we can talk about that won't end in an argument?" she asked facetiously.

"Why don't you tell me about your business?" he suggested.

She stared at him in disbelief. "No way. That's bound to cause a conflict. I already know your views on love and romance."

"That's true," he conceded. "But I'm beginning to think there may be more to your business than just hearts-and-flowers."

"There's a lot more. Weddings are big business, now more than ever. Regardless of your personal viewpoint, more and more people are choosing to get married and they're opting for large, traditional weddings."

"Which is good for business," he said perceptively.

"Of course. The woman who was in today, the one I almost lost because of that little demonstration earlier—"

"Don't remind me."

"Her wedding is probably going to reach forty thousand dollars before she's through. She's planning an enormous wedding extravaganza at the Museum of Modern Art."

He stared at her and then burst out laughing. "She's getting married in a museum?"

Her mouth twitched slightly as she tried to suppress a smile. "Yes, it's becoming quite the thing to do. There will be a five-piece band, and a luxurious buffet supper for five hundred of her closest friends. Her dress is being designed especially for her, and the bridesmaids' dresses are coming directly from Paris. Our job will be to coordinate the entire event, which includes the cake, photography, video, music, flowers, catering, limousines, party favors, wedding-party gifts, and I guess that's about it."

"I'm impressed," he said. "But I have to say I'm also a little confused. That sounds more like a circus than a wedding."

She tipped her head in acknowledgment. "It's a little too much for my taste, but as you said, to each his own. And my partner, Liz, is very happy. The entire wedding will run over forty thousand dollars and out of that we take about fifteen percent, which will definitely help our budget."

Raising his eyebrows, he shook his head in amazement. "Forty thousand dollars," he echoed. "Well, just promise me one thing."

"What's that?"

"When it's time for them to get a divorce, send them to me."

"Don't be so cynical," she chided, refusing to take offense at his obviously teasing comment.

"I'm sorry, but I don't think there's any way their marriage is going to live up to that kind of a beginning. They'll probably be fighting before the evening's over."

Their conversation was interrupted by the arrival of Sonny and two steaming plates of pasta primavera, which was just as well since their truce was a tenuous one at best. The creamy linguine covered with fresh vegetables and parmesan cheese smelled wonderful, and Kate eyed the food hungrily. Her lunch had been a cup of soup and an orange, and her stomach was grumbling noisily.

"This looks absolutely delicious." She twirled the long strands of pasta on the fork, trying to ignore the interested looks of both Barrett and Sonny, and hoping she wouldn't drop anything down the front of her dress. But once she tasted the cheesy mixture, everything else fled from her mind as she savored the delicate mingling of herbs and spices.

"This is fantastic." She smiled at the pleased expression on Sonny's face. She felt like a queen who had just conferred some great honor on a lowly subject. Sonny was obviously proud of his food.

Barrett laughed as she dug into her meal with the same enthusiastic passion she brought to everything. "I think she likes it," he said simply.

"Enjoy," Sonny replied with a happy smile, leaving them alone.

They didn't talk much for a while, content to eat in companionable silence. When they did speak it was about light, inconsequential things such as movies, books and the city. They found to their mutual surprise that they did have a few things in common. They both liked mysteries and sailing on the bay, eating lobster tails on Fisherman's Wharf and riding cable cars, a hobby that Barrett sheepishly admitted was one of his favorite pastimes.

It was a wonderful, filling meal, and after popping the last piece of French bread into her mouth, Kate sat back with a groan. She was sure she had gained at least five pounds in the past hour.

Barrett sent her a teasing smile. "You aren't a very considerate dinner partner. Most of the women I know leave half their plate for me to finish."

Kate grinned at his playful comment. "Not me. I love food, as you can probably tell."

Barrett eyed her figure with genuine approval. She was slender but not excruciatingly thin. There was nothing wrong with that body, not that he could see. In fact she was far more tempting than he would have liked. "It certainly doesn't show," he said in a deep voice.

She caught her breath at the flash of desire in his eyes. His look told her more than she wanted to know, and the lighthearted silence became oppressively heavy. She shifted her eyes uneasily, hoping her own desire was not so apparent. She was grateful when the waiter came over to take their empty plates and offer them coffee. The intrusion broke the tension that had sprung up between them.

"This was very nice," she said.

Barrett looked around at the cosy surroundings with an amused smile on his face. "It is kind of romantic. I didn't think of that when I chose it."

She couldn't resist a smile at his matter-of-fact statement. "I'm sure you didn't."

"So why hasn't the romantic atmosphere put you in a romantic mood?" he said playfully. "Here we are alone in the candlelight, a man and a woman and—"

"And twenty other people."

"I wasn't going to say that," he said, reaching out for her good hand, and gently squeezing her fingers. "Now look who isn't being romantic."

"Well this isn't supposed to be a romantic evening."

"Sometimes you don't have a choice. You just have to take the moments as they come."

"I don't know if I agree with that. Sometimes it's better to think twice before you let a moment or a mood take over your actions. The consequences can be devastating.'' Her voice was more bitter than she had intended, something she knew would not escape his eagle eye.

"There you go, being mysterious again," he said. "But I won't push you, not yet."

"I think we should get the check, it's getting late."

"Everything all right?" the waiter asked, breaking into their conversation.

"Perfect," Barrett replied, taking the check.

"Why don't we split the bill?" Kate suggested.

"No, it will be my treat. I don't expect my dates to pay for dinner."

"This isn't a date," she protested.

"Maybe not technically, but I still insist. And I must say I'm surprised at your reaction. I thought you were an old-fashioned girl."

"Believing in love and romance doesn't mean I want to push the clock back to the days when women were treated subserviently," she said fiercely.

He shook his head in amazement, and then pushed the check across the table to her. "Okay, you can pay."

She looked up at him with a startled expression. His response had caught her completely off guard, and he was enjoying her look of discomfort. Darn, why had she opened her big mouth! She had no cash, and her Visa card was almost at the limit. She let out a small breath as she saw that total was well within reach. Sonny had not charged them for the wine, and the meal was very reasonable.

"Everything okay?" Barrett asked with casual amusement. "We're not going to have to wash dishes or anything?"

She made a face at his teasing comment. "No, we're fine."

She was digging into her wallet when Sonny came over and whisked the check away. "I'm sorry, they made a mistake. Your meal is on the house," he said with a smile.

"Don't argue with him," Barrett advised. "He's very stubborn, just like you."

"That's very kind of you," Kate said, ignoring his last remark.

"I owe Barrett a lot," he said. "This is just a small token of my appreciation."

"But—"

"No arguments," he replied. "Please come again, soon."

"Thank you," Kate replied while Barrett added his own thanks.

She drew her coat tightly around her as they walked out of the restaurant. The fog had descended on the city and the moist air chilled her face as they walked down the street to the car. She tried to ignore Barrett's hand on the back of her waist. It was a simple gesture, certainly not threatening, but with him even the tiniest touch sent shivers down her spine.

Chapter Six

The ride home was swift and quiet. They had talked about so many things at dinner that they were content to just sit in silence. Despite their earlier conversation, Kate didn't really feel she knew Barrett. He had thrown out some tantalizing tidbits about his marriage and divorce but never really talked about his emotions. She had seen flickerings of pain and bitterness in his dark brown eyes, but she could only guess at the depth of those feelings.

Not that she had been much better. Despite his gentle, probing questions, she had been unable to tell him about her past, about her mother—all the reasons why she desperately wanted a romantic, loving marriage. A couple of times she had thought about opening up to him, but it was a difficult subject to bring up, and one that she wasn't particularly proud to discuss.

She had only considered it because Barrett was surprisingly easy to talk to and a good listener. It was probably this trait that made him such a successful attorney. He was an interesting blend of arrogant ruthlessness and gentle, understanding compassion.

Caught up in her thoughts, she jumped when his hand lightly touched her thigh and then blushed as she realized he was only changing gears, not making a pass. But the light touch made the cozy interior seem suffocatingly small, and she instinctively moved away until she could feel the door handle jabbing painfully into her side.

She tried to look unconcernedly out the window, but she could feel his amused glance. She was acting like a foolish teenager. But she didn't know what to do, how to act around him. That was why she hadn't confided in him. He had a side that was sensitive and kind, but he also had a mischievous side and a sensuality that was dangerously appealing.

There was a strong attraction between them. She knew that as well as he did, but what kind of a relationship could they have? They wanted different things. He was a man who wanted to seize the moment not conduct a long-term relationship. He had been married once and that was enough. She, on the other hand, wanted to get married or at least develop a long-lasting relationship that would eventually lead to marriage. At least that's what she had wanted up until a week ago, up until the time she had met Barrett.

Now she was beginning to think she didn't know what she wanted anymore. She should be out with some nice, safe man who was interested in marriage and family. But instead she had chosen to flirt with danger with a terribly sexy, determined bachelor.

"Something wrong?" Barrett asked, looking pointedly at her hands. "You've got quite a beat going there."

She looked down at her drumming fingers in dismay. "Sorry."

"This is the street, isn't it?"

"Yes, turn right. It's the mustard-colored building on the left."

Barrett pulled put in front of the building, switching on his hazard lights as he double-parked. She stepped out quickly, grateful for once that the limited parking would allow her to make a quick getaway. Unfortunately Barrett had other ideas. He followed her out of the car and up the walkway to her door.

As she put her key in the lock he unexpectedly leaned over and put his hand under her chin, turning her around to face him.

"I guess this is the moment of truth, as they call it," he said, his face just inches from her own.

Kate swallowed, her resolve flying out the window as his dark brown eyes cast a spell on her. "I don't think so."

"I do," he said softly. "I haven't been able to forget that very brief kiss we shared the other night. And I've been wanting to do it again."

Her blue eyes darkened at his provocative statement. She hadn't been able to forget that kiss, either. But that had been just an impulsive moment. Now he was giving her a chance to think as his finger caressed her cheek, his eyes gently inquisitive.

His touch was like a flame lighting up her soul, and she had to fight off the impulse to move closer to him, to reach out and run her hand through his wavy, dark hair, bringing his lips down to hers. God, what was she thinking? She couldn't have this man. She didn't want this man.

Silently she stepped out of his reach, and before he could say anything else she opened the door and slipped inside her apartment. She held her breath in expectation, a sudden ache of disappointment flooding through her as she heard his footsteps go down the walk and then the rumble of his car engine. Finally there was silence, and shaking her head she turned off the lights and headed for bed.

Unfortunately sleep evaded her, and after tossing and turning for several hours she decided to fix herself a hot cup of tea. The clock on her night table read two-fifteen, and with a groan she thrust her feet into a pair of woolly pink slippers and padded into the kitchen.

While she was waiting for the water to boil, she restlessly opened the refrigerator door and grinned as

she looked at the contents. Dare she? The half gallon
of mocha-almond-fudge was beckoning to her. It had
been left over from an engagement party she had organized the week before, and until now she had resisted one of her favorite obsessions. What the heck
she decided, reaching for the container and pulling out
a spoon. She felt like a pig, first pasta and now ice
cream. Tomorrow she would have to starve.

An hour later she felt disgustingly stuffed and less
than satisfied. She just couldn't get Barrett out of her
mind, and it was driving her crazy. He was not the
kind of man she wanted to be attracted to. He was too
blunt, too rough around the edges. Not that he didn't
dress elegantly and drive a beautiful car. It wasn't the
surface image, it was the real man. He wasn't one to
wrap up his words in a pretty package or pretend to
feel something he didn't feel. He wasn't interested in
romance or love or marriage. She knew he wanted her
physically, and Lord knows her emotions seemed to
run amok when she saw him, but that wasn't enough.
Was it?

Liz smiled politely as Kate escorted Davina Smythe
out of the office. They waited until they heard the
downstairs door slam shut and then Kate sank down
on the couch with an exhausted sigh.

"God help me. I don't think I'm going to make it
until her wedding. Six more weeks of pure torture."

Liz nodded in commiseration. "I heard her complaining about the bridesmaids' dresses. Sounded like she wanted you to resew them personally."

Kate wrinkled her nose in disgust. "Little does she know I can't even sew a hem, much less a fancy dress. But I think I calmed her down, and I talked to the woman at the bridal salon. She assured me that the seamstress would work with each girl to take in that side panel that seems to be sticking out so appallingly."

"Well, it's tough to find bridesmaids' dresses that are nice. They're only made to stay together for a six-hour period, tops. After that they start to fall apart."

Kate groaned in response. "Please don't tell Davina that." She stumbled to her feet wearily. "Thank heavens she was the last appointment. It's been a long day and a long week."

"Heard any more from Barrett Fox?" Liz asked casually.

"No," Kate said crisply. Aside from mentioning the altercation in the hallway and their dinner, she had been reluctant to discuss him with Liz. Despite their long friendship, her feelings were too raw to stand up to an objective discussion. Fortunately they had been too busy to talk about anything, and Barrett had been conspicuously absent for the last three days. That fact was both encouraging and discouraging.

"I guess you don't want to talk about it?" Liz said wisely, leaning back in her chair.

"There's nothing to talk about. We haven't seen each other since Tuesday night."

"Yes, but you still haven't told me about the dinner, and I've been very good about not asking nosy questions. But my patience just ran out."

"Nothing happened," Kate said in exasperation. "We had dinner, we talked, we argued most of the time. That was it."

"No good-night kiss or anything?"

"Definitely not."

"I wonder why?" Liz mused. "The man is obviously interested in you, and he doesn't look like the slow type to me."

Kate shook her head impatiently. "Don't be ridiculous. One dinner does not signify interest. And even if he were, I'm not."

"Why ever not?" she asked incredulously. "You've been moaning around here for months, claiming that there are no exciting, interesting men left in San Francisco. And here you are out to dinner with one of the finest-looking men I've seen in a long time, and you claim to have absolutely no interest. I don't believe it."

"Barrett Fox is not for me, Liz. He's too, too—"

"Too what? Too sexy, too good-looking?"

"Try too arrogant, too cynical and too, all right, sexy. He's not the kind of man who's interested in a long-term relationship. He was married, and he's now divorced, which makes him definitely gun-shy. The two of us are complete opposites."

"I've seen hardened bachelors succumb when they meet the right woman."

"You're a fine one to talk," Kate said indignantly. "You're a female version of Barrett Fox. You and Rick are wildly in love, but you refuse to consider marriage. Now Rick may be willing to settle for that kind of relationship, but I'm not."

"Well, fine," Liz said, somewhat offended by her remark.

"I'm sorry," Kate immediately apologized. "I didn't mean to downgrade your relationship. But it's just not for me. I understand your point of view, and I hope you can understand mine."

"I'm trying to, because in a way it helps me understand Rick. He hasn't exactly given up on the idea of marriage, either."

"Aren't you worried about getting hurt?" Kate asked with concern. "You and Rick are getting very serious about each other, and when one person wants to move ahead and the other doesn't someone is bound to get hurt."

"But we haven't lied to each other," Liz argued. "Everything has been completely open and honest."

Kate shook her head worriedly. "I still think you could be heading for another heartbreak. It's easy to talk yourself into something when you're in love, but sooner or later reality hits and sometimes it can be devastating," she said passionately, wishing she could take back her words as Liz looked at her in surprise.

An awkward silence fell on the room. "What happened, Kate?"

"Forget I said that. It's not important," Kate replied with a quick frown of dismissal. She looked down at her watch and then back at Liz who was watching her with a curious expression on her face. "I'm going to go to lunch. I need to get some air."

"I'm sorry if I upset you."

She brushed away her apology. "You didn't. My nerves are on edge. I just need to take a walk and get my energy back."

By the time she reached the bottom of the Golden Gate Bridge she was completely out of breath. The two-mile walk had done her good, and drawing her coat around her, she took a deep breath of the refreshing, windy sunshine.

Just below the Golden Gate Bridge was a vista point allowing visitors an amazing view of the spectacular bridge towering over the gateway from the Pacific Ocean to the San Francisco Bay. Today the point was crowded with tourists and lunchtime joggers, all taking advantage of the beautiful weather.

Leaning against the railing she gazed out over the bay, trying to summon up her usual enthusiasm for what she considered to be one of the prettiest spots in San Francisco. From here she had a clear view of the colorful sailboats dotting the bay, the fishing boats and the daring people on Windsurfers willing to brave the bay's cold water and risky currents.

SILHOUETTE DELIVERS FIRST-CLASS ROMANCE— DIRECT TO YOUR DOOR

Mail the Heart sticker on the postpaid order card today and you'll receive:

— 4 new Silhouette Romance™ novels—FREE
— a lovely gold-plated chain—FREE
— and a surprise mystery bonus—FREE

But that's not all. You'll also get:

FREE HOME DELIVERY

When you subscribe to Silhouette Romance™, the excitement, romance and faraway adventures of these novels can be yours for previewing in the convenience of your own home. Every month we'll deliver 6 new books right to your door. If you decide to keep them, they'll be yours for only $2.25* each and there is no extra charge for postage and handling! There is no obligation to buy—you can cancel at any time simply by writing "cancel" on your statement or by returning a shipment of books to us at our cost.

Free Monthly Newsletter

It's the indispensable insider's look at our most popular writers and their upcoming novels. Now you can have a behind-the-scenes look at the fascinating world of Silhouette! It's an added bonus you'll look forward to every month!

Special Extras—FREE

Because our home subscribers are our most valued readers, we'll be sending you additional free gifts from time to time in your monthly book shipments, as a token of our appreciation.

OPEN YOUR MAILBOX TO A WORLD OF LOVE AND ROMANCE EACH MONTH. JUST COMPLETE, DETACH AND MAIL YOUR FREE OFFER CARD TODAY!

*Terms and prices subject to change without notice. Sales tax applicable in NY and Iowa.
© 1990 HARLEQUIN ENTERPRISES LTD.

FREE-OFFER CARD

4 FREE BOOKS

FREE GOLD-PLATED CHAIN

FREE MYSTERY BONUS

PLACE HEART STICKER HERE

FREE-HOME DELIVERY

FREE FACT-FILLED NEWSLETTER

MORE SURPRISES THROUGHOUT THE YEAR—FREE

☑ **YES!** Please send me four Silhouette Romance™
novels, free, along with my free gold-plated chain and
my free mystery gift as explained on the opposite page.

215 CIS HAYT
(U-SIL-R-08/90)

NAME _____

ADDRESS _____ APT. _____

CITY _____ STATE _____

ZIP CODE _____

Remember! To receive your free books, gold-plated chain and mystery gift, return the postpaid card below. But don't delay!

DETACH AND MAIL CARD TODAY!

If offer card is missing, write to:
Silhouette Books, 901 Fuhrmann Blvd., P.O. Box 1867, Buffalo, NY 14269-1867

MAIL THE POSTPAID CARD TODAY!

BUSINESS REPLY CARD

FIRST CLASS MAIL   PERMIT NO. 717   BUFFALO, NY

POSTAGE WILL BE PAID BY ADDRESSEE

SILHOUETTE BOOKS
901 FUHRMANN BLVD
PO BOX 1867
BUFFALO NY 14240-9952

NO POSTAGE
NECESSARY
IF MAILED
IN THE
UNITED STATES

In the distance the daunting island fortress of Alcatraz loomed alarmingly out of the water. Once the home of some of the most dangerous criminals in the country, the island prison was now abandoned and only open to the public for guided tours. Kate had taken one of those tours during her first couple of months in the city, and although impressed by the history of the prison she had been grateful to leave the dark, dungeon-like rooms for the unrestricted freedom of the city.

Shaking her head, she felt suddenly constricted and she pulled the combs out of her hair, enjoying the sense of freedom as she gazed into the turbulent water below. She felt a sense of affinity with the water, the waves crashing out of control against the rocks below, the wind whipping in all directions. She had felt that same turbulence since meeting Barrett. Her nice, easygoing existence had been blown out of control, and while part of her longed for a return to normality, another part of her embraced the exiting feelings Barrett aroused in her.

Her attraction to him was as old as time. Two people meet, kiss and fall in love. No, she shook her head. She was not going to fall in love with a man who didn't believe in love.

Sighing deeply she stood at the railing, lost in thought, her mind drifting back to another time.

She had been thirteen years old when she had first learned the truth about her mother and father. It had taken her completely by surprise. Nestled in the warm cocoon of her grandparents' home in Mendocino, she had never thought much about the man who was her father. He had died before she was born, and her grandparents had helped her mother to raise her.

But the secret eventually came out, as most secrets do, at a time when she was particularly vulnerable. Adolescence, a period of life that she never wanted to go through again. All of her insecurities and awkwardness were suddenly heightened by the realization that she was a bastard child, illegitimate. She knew the slang words. She had heard every one in a heated confrontation with another child.

Angry and betrayed, she had gone first to her grandparents. They were the stable force in her life, the people she had always trusted. They told her the truth. Her mother and father had met at a summer art festival, both young and restless. They fell in love, they made a child, but they never married. When the summer was over, her father had disappeared.

It sounded so simple, so straightforward, but even at thirteen she had realized there was more to the story. She had wanted answers, explanations, but the only one who could give them to her refused to talk. Her mother and she had never been close, but the shocking news of her birth drove a wedge deeper between them.

The hidden anger and resentment festered inside both of them. She withdrew from her mother, attaching herself to her grandparents, while her mother sought refuge in the company of men, lots and lots of men.

Her grandparents tried desperately to bridge the gap between the two of them. But their efforts were futile, and when they were unexpectedly killed in an automobile accident the final tie between Kate and her mother was broken. She had been nineteen then, and she had made her way on her own, traveling to San Francisco, working her way through school and eventually setting up her own business.

She didn't think much about the past except when she met a man. That's when the pain started again. She was afraid to trust anyone, frightened that she might fall in love with the wrong man, that she might end up like her mother.

No, it wasn't going to happen. She knew what she wanted out of life, a relationship like her grandparents had had, filled with love and laughter and romance. Her face softened as she remembered their long, devoted love affair.

But that was all in the past. Her grandparents were gone. Her mother was as good as gone. She had only herself to worry about, and her business. The thought of business brought her rushing back to the present. She looked at her watch with a groan. It was after two. She had been gone three hours. Liz was probably frantic. She had never done anything so irresponsible before, just walking out and leaving everything up in the air.

She immediately headed back to work, the physical exertion and the warm, sunny day driving the bad memories out of her mind.

Mr. Ramoni waved to her as she went by. His flower cart was crowded with people, and he sent her a beaming smile. She smiled back as she saw the woman standing next to him was his beloved Elena.

A couple of months back he had mentioned that now that their kids were grown and gone, he and his wife were having trouble readjusting, getting used to being by themselves. That's when she had offered her romantic remedy. But watching them together, she couldn't take all the credit. They belonged together. They had just needed time to remember what had brought them together in the first place.

She jogged up the stairs to her office and jumped back as the door swung open, nearly knocking her down.

"There you are," Barrett announced, looking somewhat annoyed and perhaps a little concerned.

She stared at him in surprise. "Were you looking for me?"

"Yes. And your partner is worried sick. She said you went out for a walk a couple of hours ago."

"I just needed a break," she explained, wondering why he looked so tense. He couldn't possibly have been worried about her. "Did you want to see me about something?"

He smiled to himself at her words. "You could say that."

She looked at him warily. "What's wrong now? I already told you I'm not taking down the wallpaper."

"You won't have to. My crew is going to handle that tomorrow," he replied. "But before you start arguing, let me assure you that the replacement wallpaper will be very nice, and not in any way austere. In fact I left a sample with your partner, and she was very pleased with it."

Kate shrugged her shoulders. "Apparently I don't have much to say about it, anyway."

"That's never stopped you before."

"I'm not in the mood for an argument," she said.

"Something is wrong. What happened? Did that client of yours call her wedding off?"

She looked at him blankly. "Courtney? No. At least I don't think so."

"Good. I was afraid she might have been upset about that scene she witnessed."

"No, everything is fine. I told you I just needed a break. It happens every now and then. A breath of fresh air, and I'm ready to go again."

"Good," he said with satisfaction. "In that case are you free for dinner tonight?"

"Dinner?"

"Yes, you know the meal that you eat around six o'clock."

"I know what it is. I was just thinking about my schedule," she prevaricated.

"Oh, prior engagement?"

"No, but I'm not very hungry."

"Well, it's only three o'clock, maybe you'll be hungry later. Or is that just a tactful way of saying no, thank you."

She shook her head in amazement. "Most men would just take it as a no and forget about it. What is it with you, anyway? I'm sure you've got dozens of women dying to go out with you."

"Yes, but I don't want them, I want you."

She felt an unwelcome surge of excitement at his words. It would be so easy to say yes, but she didn't think she could handle another evening of soft lights, good food and Barrett.

"I just don't feel like going to a fancy restaurant," she said finally, searching for a good reason. "I spend so much time in that kind of atmosphere that I like to get away from it when I'm off work."

He nodded his head agreeably. "That's fine with me. I'd invite you to my house, but I'm sure you'd say no," he added quickly as she opened her mouth to protest. "So we'll go someplace that will be a nice change of pace for you. Actually it was my first choice, but knowing you, I thought you'd prefer a night of dinner and dancing."

"What are you talking about now?"

"You'll see. I'll pick you up at six-thirty. Dress casually and warm. By that I mean down jacket, if you have one."

"Wait a second," she protested as he hurried down the steps. "I want to know what you're talking about."

He paused at the bottom, but he wasn't listening to her, his gaze was fixed on a slender young woman walking up to greet him.

"Hi, Barry," the young girl said cheekily reaching up to give him a hug.

"Where the hell have you been?" he growled.

"I thought you would be pleased to see me. And you haven't introduced me to your friend," she added, pointing to Kate.

Kate started as they turned to her. "I'm sorry, I didn't mean to stare."

"That's okay," Barrett replied, pulling the younger woman to his side.

Kate felt a sudden stabbing pain as he casually ruffled the other woman's hair. What was going on here? Who was this woman looking so comfortably ensconced in Barrett's embrace?

"I should go back to work."

"No, wait. I want to introduce you to my sister. This is Sarah. This is Kate Marlowe. She owns the wedding agency upstairs." He smiled to himself as the tension in Kate's face eased. A little jealousy was always a good sign.

"It's nice to meet you," Kate replied. "But I thought you were much younger for some reason."

"Probably because Barrett still thinks of me as a fourteen-year-old," Sarah wisecracked. "Actually I'm twenty-two years old and quite capable of handling my own life."

"That's still up for debate," Barrett replied. "Now I want to know where you've been for the last two days and why you left me some skimpy note saying not to worry."

"I'd rather hear about Miss Marlowe's business," Sarah said, turning to Kate with the same lazy smile as her brother. "I'm very interested in weddings at the moment."

"Why is that?" Barrett demanded suspiciously.

Kate looked from one to the other with a confused expression on her face. Obviously there was more going on here than was known to her.

"I have to go," she said again, breaking into their conversation. "I'm sorry that I don't have time to talk right now, but I need to get back to work."

"That's okay," Sarah replied. "I'll come and talk to you sometime when you're free."

"First you'll talk to me," Barrett said, pushing her toward his office. "Oh, and Kate, don't forget six-thirty."

She shook her head as he shut the door. Why hadn't she just said no? A simple little word, but she just couldn't get it out. A small smile curved her lips as she remembered the tender look in his eyes, and she went back to work in a much better frame of mind.

Chapter Seven

Barrett was humming lightly under his breath as he maneuvered his Mercedes through the heavy Friday-night traffic. He grinned as Kate sent him another covert look from under her long black lashes. She was pretending to be unconcerned, but he knew her imagination was running wild. He hadn't had this much fun in years. There was something about her that was very, very special.

"Would you please shut up," she said with mock annoyance. "That humming is driving me crazy, especially since I can't figure out what song it's supposed to be."

He patted one jean-clad thigh reassuringly. "Don't worry, you'll know soon enough."

"I really couldn't care less," she drawled. "I'm sure wherever we're going will be fine." She stared out at the passing traffic idly. "Your sister seemed very nice."

"She's a handful. She took off Tuesday, left me a note about going to Lake Tahoe with some friends and that was it. No phone calls, nothing."

She laughed at his chagrined expression. "You sound like a disgruntled little boy."

"I can't help it. I've been taking care of her for the last eight years, and just because she insists she is now an adult I can't stop worrying about her."

"No, I don't suppose you can," she said softly, touched by his obvious devotion.

"But she's got a mind of her own, stubborn as hell."

"Takes after you, does she?"

He smiled at her teasing comment. "Unfortunately yes. And I think I've got some big problems coming up. She told me today that she's in love with some guy named Jeff, and that she's thinking about marriage."

"Well, that's only natural," Kate pointed out. "Lots of girls that age think about marriage, especially when they've met someone special."

"She's too young to get married," he growled.

"How old were you? Twenty-three, twenty-four?"

"Twenty-four, but that was different," he said defensively. "I was much more worldly than Sarah. She's grown up in a very sheltered environment, and to top it off she's going to be a very rich young lady.

I'm afraid someone is going to take advantage of her vulnerability. I just don't know what I'm going to do. Do you have any ideas?''

Kate was touched by the worry in his dark brown eyes, and for the first time she noticed the faint shadings of gray in his hair. It must have been very difficult raising his sister all alone.

"Kate? What do you think I should do?"

"I don't know," she said slowly. "You know Sarah much better than I do. Maybe you don't have to do anything. Just be there for her, and by that I mean be willing to listen to her side, have an open mind. After all this guy may be just right for her."

"I should have expected an answer like that from you. I'm sure you've never talked anyone out of marriage."

"Well, why would I?" she asked in exasperation. "Marriage is my business. I happen to believe in the institution." She paused, "And from where I sit you don't really have much choice, anyway. Your sister can do whatever she pleases. She is an adult."

"There's no way I'm going to let her ruin her life," he said firmly. "All the romantic reasons in the world are not going to change my mind. Regardless of what she thinks, she can't live on love, and at the moment I control the money."

His face took on an expression of pure arrogance, and she shook her head in disgust. Every time she began to think he was a nice guy, his ego stepped in. "You know I really don't know why you asked me out tonight or why I agreed to come. We spend every minute arguing."

"I'd rather think of it as a spirited discussion," he said, wheedling a reluctant smile out of her. "I admit I'm a little opinionated, but you certainly manage to hold your own. And despite our differences, I respect your judgment. You're the kind of woman I'd like my sister to be—beautiful, intelligent, independent and single."

"What about romantic?" she asked dryly, trying not to show how pleased she was by his compliment. "Don't bother. I already know the answer." She looked out the window as the traffic began to thin, now that they were further out of the city. "Where are we going?"

"We're here," he said with a smile, putting on his signal light as he pulled over.

"Where's here?" she asked, looking at the bay on one side and an industrial development on the other.

"Candlestick Park. The Giants play the Dodgers tonight. It should be a great game."

She looked at him in amazement. "Baseball? You're taking me to a baseball game? I thought we were going to dinner."

"We are. They have terrific hot dogs here, and if you're a good girl I'll buy you an ice-cream cone for dessert."

"I can't believe you're taking me to a baseball game."

"You're the one who said she was tired of fancy restaurants. I just try to please my dates."

"Right. You had tickets for this all along," she accused.

He grinned in response. "Of course I did. I never miss the Giants playing the Dodgers. You do like baseball, don't you?"

"What if I didn't?" Actually she loved baseball, and had become a genuine Giants fan since moving to the city.

"I can still turn the car around," he offered, casting her a speculative look. "We can change clothes, dine at the Top of the Mark, dance to soft music, go back to your apartment and—"

She frowned at his wicked expression. "I think we better stick to baseball. The only scoring going on tonight will be the Giants."

"Ouch," he laughed. "I'm beginning to think I made the wrong choice."

They joined the steady stream of cars entering the park, and Barrett dug through his wallet for his reserved-parking pass. "I have season tickets," he explained at her questioning glance.

"At least we're going first-class," she said dryly.

"Only the best for you, sweet Kate."

"I think you're the one who's used to getting what you want."

He laughed softly, sending her a penetrating glance. "If that were true we'd be making love right now, instead of going to a baseball game."

Her heart skipped a beat as his eyes darkened invitingly. "In fact that can still be arranged."

She stared at him in amazement. "You never give up, do you?"

"Not when it's something this important," he replied seriously. "Come on, let's go find our seats."

Their seats were directly behind home plate and about ten rows back, offering them one of the best views of the game. True to his word, Barrett bought her not only hot dogs but also popcorn, nachos with cheese and a chocolate malt. She couldn't believe the enormous amount of food they both consumed, but there was something about the ballpark and the cold night that made her ravenous.

The game was close, with lots of hitting and scoring, but if the truth were told, Kate was more interested in watching Barrett than anyone else. She liked seeing him so happy, so carefree, and when he put his arm around her and tossed a blanket over them she made no protest. When the fog rolled in during the eighth inning, covering the stadium in misty moisture, she had no complaints, not snuggled up in Barrett's arms. In fact she was somewhat disappointed when the game ended.

Apparently Barrett felt the same way, suggesting that they stop for a drink on their way home. Pushing aside her cautiousness she agreed, and they spent another two hours arguing good-naturedly about baseball. It wasn't until they were driving back to her apartment that the nervousness returned.

"I'll see you in," Barrett offered. "It's late."

He put an arm around her shoulders as they walked up to her door, waiting patiently as she slipped her key into the lock.

"It looks like you did some housecleaning," he teased, as she turned on the lights.

"I finished a few projects," she admitted. "But I'm afraid I like clutter. Knickknacks and souvenirs, ruffles and lace make me feel warm and comfortable."

"I know what you mean. This place is more than an apartment, it's a home."

"Yes, it is," she said simply, standing still in the middle of the room. "I like feeling settled."

"That's a strange word, settled." His eyes darkened with some unknown emotion.

"Is it? Don't you want to feel settled?"

He shook his head. "No, I don't think so. I like changes, adventures. I think you do, too."

"Yes, but when the adventures are over, I like to go home."

"You're still an intriguing woman. I can't quite figure you out, so independent, strong and yet incredibly soft." His voice lingered on the last word, sending a shiver down her spine.

"I think I like being mysterious," she replied, folding her arms protectively in front of her. He suddenly looked predatory.

"You do, huh?" He took a deliberate step toward her. "There's one problem with being a lady of mystery, though."

"What's that?'' she whispered, as he moved closer to her, a wicked glint in his eyes.

"I'm never sure of your reaction, so I just have to take my chances. For instance," he paused, his breath fanning her cheek, "a good-night kiss is usually appropriate, but with you I'm not sure I wouldn't get slapped across the face."

His lips were so close, she thought he would kiss her before she could reply, but he waited. Her nerves screamed with anticipation.

"Maybe you should try it and see," she said, refusing to take responsibility but still wanting.

She watched in fascination as his lips curved into a smile, revealing a set of brilliant white teeth. Everything about the man was perfect except for his teasing attitude.

"Maybe you should start," he suggested, grasping her shoulders lightly. His touch burned through her knit sweater and her own hands instinctively responded, drifting up his arms and around his neck. She looked into his eyes, the lightness fading as she moved closer into his arms. "Or maybe I should just take my chances," he growled, bending his head.

His lips touched hers in a long, hot kiss that sent her senses spinning out of control. He kissed her hungrily, and she responded in kind. She couldn't think of anything but the delicious taste of his mouth, the rough edges of his cheek and the warm male scent of his body. When he started to pull away she unconsciously protested, burying her hands in the thick waves of his hair, pulling his head back down to her. They kissed again and again, long, deep kisses that seemed to touch her soul. Finally they broke away, breathless.

Barrett stared down at her in fascination. He had never felt so much desire from a kiss, a simple caress. "Kate," he breathed.

She licked her lips, not knowing what to say. Words seemed so meaningless now. She dropped her eyes, preferring the safety of his buttoned-down shirt to the sensuous invitation in his dark brown eyes.

"I guess we should say good-night," she said.

His hands abruptly dropped to his sides, leaving her feeling cold and lonely. His silence forced her to look back up at him.

"Are you sure you want to say good-night?" he asked, a touch of lightness returning to his manner. "I thought we were just getting to know each other."

"It's late."

"It's early," he parried.

"I'm tired."

"I feel wide-awake."

"Barrett stop, please. Can't you take no for an answer?" she complained, trying not to smile.

"I haven't heard the word no, yet," he argued. "Just some silly excuses trying to cover up what just happened. It wasn't so bad, you know. In fact it was very, very nice."

She couldn't stop the rosy flush that spread across her cheeks any more than she could stop herself from wanting him, and the intensity of her feelings both excited and frightened her. She turned away, trying to hide what he already knew, that she was incredibly susceptible to his charm.

"Barrett, please, I'm asking you to go," she stated quietly and firmly.

He studied her tense shoulders thoughtfully, and made a decision. "Okay. I'm going. But I had a great time tonight. I hope you did, too."

She turned back to face him, surprised by his sensitivity. He wasn't going to push. She was grateful for the reprieve. "I had a wonderful time," she admitted.

"Good. Then I have a suggestion to make."

Her guard flew back into place, but she managed a pleasant smile.

"Let's spend time together. See if we can find something to agree on. What do you say?"

"I don't know if that's possible."

"Stop arguing. Say yes," he commanded. "Just think, it's a perfect opportunity for you to convert me into a romantic. Look at it as a challenge."

She threw up her hands in defeat. The man had all the right answers. "Okay. We'll be friends." She stuck out her hand. "Shake on it?"

"Is that your best offer?"

"I'm afraid so."

He solemnly stuck out his hand and gave her hand a gentle squeeze. "When's our next date? Tomorrow?"

"I have a wedding tomorrow, the hot-air balloon launch I told you about."

"Right. I'll be interested to hear how that one comes out," he replied, walking over to the door.

"Why don't you come?" she asked impulsively, her words surprising her as much as him.

"Is that allowed?"

"Sure. I'll be running around beforehand. But once they go up, everything will be done. Then there's just a few details to take care of at the reception." She shrugged her shoulders. "If you're busy though, it's no big deal."

"Yes," he said aloud.

"Yes, you're busy?"

"No I'm not busy, and yes I'd like to come. What time?"

"Seven-thirty. The launch is at eleven. But it's in Napa, and I need to get there an hour ahead of time."

He looked at his watch with a groan. "That's about five hours from now."

"Still want to come?"

"I'll be here," he drawled, leaning over to kiss her cheek. "Sweet dreams, Kate."

"Good night," she said, closing the door gently behind him. She smiled to herself as she heard him whistling down the walkway. She felt as if she were on the verge of something terribly exciting. She couldn't wait to see him again.

Chapter Eight

Jonathan and Sandra Delaney successfully tied the knot at one thousand feet with the minister, best man and maid of honor in the balloon and a hundred cheering friends waiting on the ground below. After the ceremony and balloon ride, the wedding party adjourned to a large restaurant a few miles away for lunch and the more traditional elements of dancing, toasts and wedding cake.

Barrett had been a good sport throughout. He had greeted her at seven-thirty sharp with hot coffee and warm croissants which scored big points in her book. He hadn't uttered one word of complaint when she ran around like a madwoman the hour before the launch, trying to find a Bible the minister had forgotten to bring with him. He hadn't even complained when she dragged him through the receiving line at the restaurant or made him hold the lights for the videographer whose partner was suddenly taken ill. No, all in all he had been a terrific sport. Not one wisecrack about romance in the last six hours. Maybe there was hope for him yet.

She looked around the crowded restaurant, wondering where he had disappeared to.

"Are we almost done?" he whispered into her ear, sneaking up from behind.

She smiled as his lips brushed her neck in a feathery kiss. "Yes. That's it. They'll probably party for another hour, but we can go."

"Good, I don't know how you do it. I get tired just watching you run around. Every time I looked for you, you were in a different place solving some minor crisis."

"It can get pretty hectic," she agreed, linking her arm with his. "We can slip out if you want."

He sent her a sexy smile. "Good, let's go someplace quiet where we can be alone. All this hugging and kissing has made me very hungry."

She looked at him in surprise. "I thought you ate lunch."

"I'm not talking about lunch," he drawled.

She rolled her eyes as his meaning hit home. "Behave yourself, please."

"What do you think I've been doing all day?" he complained. "I'll go get the car and meet you out front."

She nodded and watched him stroll through the restaurant. He was such a good-looking man, tall and powerfully built, and Kate had noticed more than one admiring glance going his way. But he was oblivious to the attention. In fact he seemed more at ease chatting with the men than with the women.

"Miss Marlowe?"

"Yes, Sandra," she said, turning to the bride with a cheerful smile.

"I just wanted to thank you again. Everything was wonderful."

"I'm glad," Kate replied, squeezing her hand. "I'm going to go now, since everything is under control."

"Okay. I hope you'll thank your handsome partner. He really helped out a lot."

"He's actually just a friend, but I'll let him know. I hope you'll call me when you get back from your honeymoon and let me know how everything is going, and then we can discuss when you'll get your pictures and that sort of thing."

"Okay. Thanks again."

Kate watched Sandra's husband drag her away with a possessive smile and a kiss. That was what she loved most about her business, the happiness and joy that resulted from all her work.

"Kate," Barrett called from just inside the door.

"Coming," she replied, gathering her things together hurriedly. She had a feeling Barrett's patience was just about to run out.

* * *

Twenty miles and he hadn't said a word. He just kept looking at her with a knowing smile. It was driving her crazy.

"Okay, out with it, she commanded.

"What?" he asked innocently.

"Whatever it is that's making you smile every five minutes."

"Oh that." He paused, sending her another lazy smile. "I was just thinking about you."

"And that's amusing you?"

"Not exactly. I was just thinking about that outlandish wedding ceremony this morning and wondering if that's what you had in mind for yourself."

Somehow she didn't believe him, but for the moment she didn't feel like pushing the issue.

"I don't want to get married in a balloon," she said after a moment. "That's a little too adventurous for me."

"I'm glad to hear that."

"Why, worried I might talk you into something?" she asked playfully.

"Maybe I'm afraid I'll talk myself into something," he said under his breath.

"What?"

"Nothing. So what do you have in mind?"

"Probably something simple but beautiful. I want to be married in a church, and I'd like a very intimate gathering."

"Not five hundred people?"

"Definitely not. Maybe fifty, tops. I don't have a large family, although it would depend somewhat on my husband." She paused, lost in thought. "I'd like to be married in the evening, with a candlelight ceremony and a late supper afterwards."

"That sounds nice," he replied. "And what kind of man do you have in mind for your husband?"

She shook her head. "I don't know. I don't really have anyone in mind."

He looked at her in disbelief. "You must have some idea of what you're looking for in a husband. Let's see. You probably want someone who works nine-to-five, sends you roses and little doodads every day, writes poetry and sings love songs, someone like that, huh?"

"I didn't say that," she answered, staring out the window. He was only teasing, but his comments made her seem so artificial. "I'll admit that I like that sort of thing, but love is more important than any phony romanticism." She turned to face him. "What about you?"

"Me? I'm not looking for a wife."

"That's right. You want to go through life alone."

"Sometimes even when you're married, you're alone," he said bitterly. "Being alone isn't so bad, it's having your dreams trampled on that really kills you."

"Your first marriage was pretty bad."

"Horrible," he admitted. "Not that it was all Caroline's fault. We were both excited about the idea of being married, but we were looking at it from two different points of view. I liked the idea of being a husband, taking care of my wife, having a family. Caroline wanted to be social and travel. She really didn't have interests besides parties and clothes. It was just a matter of time before things began to break. When my parents died, it was the last straw. She gave me an ultimatum, Sarah or her."

"And you chose Sarah," she said softly.

"Of course. I love my sister very much, and I've never regretted it for one instant." He smiled to himself. "I take that back. The slumber party with twenty fifteen-year-old girls and a gang of boys who crashed the party in their boxer shorts just about did me in."

Kate grinned. "I'm sure you handled it fine."

"Well, the first thing I did was get rid of the boys. The next thing I did was order ten large pizzas. I stuffed them with so much food, they didn't have time to get into any more trouble."

"That must have been difficult for you, raising a young girl all alone. I'm sure Sarah must have put a crimp in your social life."

He shook his head. "In the beginning I was fed up with women. I wanted nothing to do with them, so it was easy to have Sarah as an excuse. And we had a good time together. I'm sure I wasn't a great father figure. I didn't know a thing about all that teenage-girl stuff. But we learned to put up with each other. She taught me a lot."

"I'm sure you did just fine. But now Sarah is a grown woman, maybe soon to be a married woman. What are you going to do with your life?"

"At the moment I'd like to spend some time with you."

"Some time?" she asked hesitantly.

He paused for so long she began to wonder if he had heard her question. "I told you last night that I'd like to get to know you better."

"Yes, you did. But I'm wondering why. We're very different people. I don't think we want the same things out of life."

Barrett sighed, as he watched the traffic through the rearview mirror. He wasn't sure what he wanted anymore. He just knew he didn't want to let Kate slip away. "We don't have to make any decisions right now, do we?"

"No, of course not. But Barrett, you have to know that I believe very strongly in love and marriage going together. I won't change my mind about that. I've seen what can happen when there is no commitment."

He looked at her in surprise. The vehemence in her voice told him that she was reacting to more than just him. He put on his signal light and pulled off at the next exit. It was time to get a few answers.

"Where are we going?" she asked curiously.

"We're going to have a serious conversation, and I can't do that while I'm driving," he said, turning into a parking space next to the harbor.

"What do you want to talk about?"

"You and your past. No more lady of mystery, Kate. I want to know what happened."

A shiver ran down her spine. "What do you mean?"

"Don't stall. There must have been a man somewhere who left you or hurt you. Your feelings about love and marriage are very strong. Talk to me."

His gentle command made her smile. He was used to getting his own way even when he was trying to be understanding.

"It really isn't that earth-shattering."

"Why don't you let me be the judge of that. Go on, start at the beginning."

"That's the only place I could start," she said, pausing for a long moment. "I'm illegitimate, Barrett, born of two people who didn't take the trouble to marry. My father disappeared a few weeks before I was born. There was nothing holding him, not even a piece of paper." She took a deep breath. "I know that being born out of wedlock isn't as important as it used to be, but it still matters to me."

Her eyes clouded over as the memories enfolded her. "My mother said he was an artist, just passing through Mendocino. It was the early sixties, and I suppose free love was fairly rampant, especially in an art community. She said they were in love, but I find that a little hard to believe. It's probably just as well. He doesn't sound like the kind of person I'd want to have as a father." She'd told herself that hundreds of times.

Barrett sat quietly, watching the emotions flit through her eyes. She didn't have to tell him that she felt betrayed, unloved, unsure—he could see it in the darkening hue of her blue eyes. He wanted to say something. But he wanted it to be the right thing, so he waited and he listened.

"I didn't have a bad childhood, actually," she continued. "My grandparents pretty much raised me. They were a wonderful, old-fashioned couple. I got a lot of my romantic ideas from watching them. They were married fifty years when they died. And they went together in an automobile accident. In some ways it seemed appropriate. I couldn't imagine one without the other."

Her eyes grew misty as she remembered her last conversation with her grandparents. She had been an angry, confused teenager, and they had been so patient with her. They had tried to understand, and they had tried to make her understand that what had happened all those years ago was something she had to forgive, to let go of. But that was an impossible thought. She couldn't just forget about her birth, suddenly stop wondering what kind of a father she had or why he hadn't wanted to love her.

After a moment she looked over at Barrett. He was so quiet, so still. She didn't know what else to say.

"Have you ever heard from him?" he asked, staring out at the bay. "Your father?"

"No. I don't suppose I ever will. My mother refuses to talk about him. I'm not sure why. I used to think it was because she had loved him so much that his leaving was just too painful to talk about. But I don't know. My mother hasn't exactly been mourning for the last twenty-five years. In fact she's quite the social butterfly, not at all like me. She's very sophisticated and charming, and she still doesn't give a damn about conventions. She changes men as often as the seasons and travels all over the world. She never married. She says she's happy. I guess she is."

"But you don't approve of her life-style," Barrett commented.

"It really isn't up to me to approve or disapprove. She's her own person. We haven't really been close, not in a very long time. We only see each other a few times a year. She travels, and once in a while we both meet at my grandparents' house in Mendocino. We've kept the house as kind of a refuge, or maybe because it's our only tie to each other. Neither one of us wants to feel all alone."

Kate leaned her head back against the seat, feeling emotionally spent. "Now you know all my deep, dark secrets, why I feel so strongly about love and marriage," she said quietly. "I've seen both sides and I know what I want, something like my grandparents had, something strong and enduring. I want commitment and all the legal ties that go along with it. I want a husband who wants the same things I do."

Barrett drummed his fingers restlessly against the steering wheel. Every word seemed to be driving them further apart. He had wanted all those things once, and he had had them, but the fairy tale had turned into a nightmare. He didn't know if he could do it again. He didn't know if he wanted to.

He frowned at her stony expression. She wasn't going to give an inch. Having heard the brief sketching of her past he understood why, but he still felt like shaking her. She saw everything as black-and-white when there were hundreds of shades of gray. She had seen two extreme sides of love, her grandparents' fifty-year marriage and her mother's open-ended life-style. But there were so many other kinds of relationships.

"Has there ever been someone serious in your life, a man you wanted to marry?" he questioned.

She shook her head. "No. I've dated, of course. But I can usually tell pretty quickly if it's going to work."

"And if it's not going to lead to marriage, you cut it off," he finished.

"I haven't met the right person yet."

"Maybe you just don't know it."

"I assume you're talking about yourself."

He banged his fist on the steering wheel. "Yes, dammit. I'm talking about me, about us." He shook his head in exasperation. "I happen to think we have something good going on between us. We can talk to each other, we can listen. That's important."

"Yes, but what I'm hearing just makes me realize that this could never work. You're a cynic. You don't believe in love. I do."

"I did believe in love," he corrected, looking grim. "I wanted all that happily-ever-after stuff as much as you do right now. But then I got married, and life became a living hell. I suddenly didn't know the woman I had married. I felt trapped, caught up in a web of things I didn't want to do, people I didn't want to be with and a woman I didn't love anymore. It was a terrible feeling, almost as if the breath was slowly being squeezed out of me.''

She stared at him in shock. She could feel his pain as clearly as if it were her own. Reaching out her hand, she touched his arm. His eyes met hers in a long, penetrating glance. She pulled her hand away and nervously straightened her skirt. "I guess there's nothing else to say.''

"I'm not so sure about that," he said. "You make me want to forget everything that happened in the past. You make me want to believe again.''

"I'm not trying to change you.''

"I know. And that alone makes me want to kiss you until you're breathless, until you run out of reasons to argue with me. Because dammit, Kate, I don't think I can walk away from you.''

"Then maybe I should walk away from you.''

The smile didn't quite reach his eyes. "You can try.'' He turned the key in the ignition and got back on the freeway. They didn't speak the rest of the way home. There didn't seem to be anything left to say.

Despite Barrett's challenging words, he was conspicuously absent during the next two weeks. She had half expected him to pursue her at every opportunity, but he didn't. Fortunately Kate was too busy to worry about it. The spring rush was on, and they were working ten- and twelve-hour days just trying to keep up with the influx of new clients and prepare for their final bridal show of the year, a wedding extravaganza at the San Francisco Hilton Hotel.

The days flew by, and aside from a few bittersweet glances of Barrett coming in and out of the office, Kate saw nothing of the man who had turned her life upside down. He called a few times, but she was always out or tied up in a meeting. She didn't call him back. She was trying to do what she had promised, walk away. And at that moment it didn't seem to be that difficult.

There were no further arguments between them. The clients going in and out of both offices were quiet and unobtrusive. There were no strange coincidences, no nasty cat fights in the hallways, no reason for Kate and Barrett to have anything to do with each other, until fate intervened once again.

Chapter Nine

"Kate," Liz called, popping her head into the inner office. "You've got a visitor, do you have a minute?"

Kate made a face and pointed at the stacks of contracts on her desk. "Who is it?"

"Sarah Fox. She said you mentioned she could stop by sometime, but if you're too busy now, she can come back. I already told her we have the show on Sunday."

"It's okay, I can take a short break," Kate replied, her curiosity taking precedence.

She stood up as Sarah waltzed into the room with a wide, enthusiastic smile on her face.

"Hello, I hope I'm not interrupting anything."

Kate shook her head with a warm smile. Sarah's brash charm reminded her of Barrett. These were two people used to getting what they wanted out of life.

"Please sit down."

Sarah sank down into the leather chair with an easy grace, crossing her slender legs in front of her. Her short denim skirt and embroidered blouse matched her slightly unorthodox personality. Kate was immediately charmed. She was open and outgoing. And so much like Barrett, the same big brown eyes and engaging smile. But there was a softness about her that Barrett lacked, an idealism and a zest for living that he had long since forgotten.

"What can I do for you?" Kate enquired.

"I'm getting married, and I'd like to hire your services," Sarah said, grinning at the startled look that flashed through Kate's eyes. "Everyone seems to have the same reaction when I say that."

"Pardon me?"

"When I told Barrett I was getting married he just stared at me, completely speechless. I don't know why it's such a surprise. Didn't I mention it when we first met?"

"Yes, of course," Kate said. "But I guess I am a little surprised."

"That's okay. It took me a while to get used to the idea, and I'm afraid Barrett is still fuming about it. But I'm sure he'll come around."

"You sound very confident," Kate remarked, remembering Barrett's strong feelings on the subject of his sister's marriage.

She tossed her short brown hair carelessly. "I guess I am. You see, I know my brother, and even though he is stubborn as hell he's also fair, and I'm sure that once he gets to know Jeff he'll be happy for us." She paused. "Barrett has this problem with the idea of marriage. He was married and divorced, and ever since then he seems to be a little down on the idea."

"Yes, he told me a bit about that," Kate admitted, twirling her pencil idly. She wondered how Barrett was taking the news. Somehow she didn't think it was going to go as easily as Sarah anticipated.

"He told you about Caroline?" Sarah echoed in amazement. "I thought there was something going on between you two."

Kate shook her head hastily. "No, no, it's not what you think. We just got into a debate one night about my business and his business, and he told me a little bit about his past. That's all."

Sarah looked at her in disbelief. "I'm still surprised. Barrett doesn't tell anyone about Caroline."

"Have you set a wedding day?" Kate asked, hoping to dampen the speculation running through Sarah's dark eyes.

"Yes, August second. That gives us three months to plan everything." She smiled eagerly. "I want a big wedding with all the trimmings, no skimping. I want a huge church with a long aisle, and a white gown with a train that goes on forever." She laughed joyously at the thought. "And of course flowers and music and a band for dancing and—"

"Slow down," Kate said with a smile. Sarah could certainly teach Barrett a thing or two about romance. "First of all, have you talked to any churches about that date?"

"No," Sarah replied. "Is that a problem?"

"That depends on where you want to get married, but that is the first step. The second major step is to decide where you want to hold the reception. I have to warn you that both churches and reception halls book up months in advance, sometimes a full year. Three months is probably not realistic if you want a full-scale wedding, especially at this time of year. Some girls have been planning their August weddings since last August," she explained.

"Really?" Sarah asked in surprise. "I thought three months would be plenty of time. In fact Jeff didn't want to wait that long."

"Most bridegrooms don't. But don't count it out yet. We haven't looked into anything, and maybe we'll get lucky." She paused for a moment, rifling through her desk drawer for her bridal packet. She pulled out the folder and handed it to Sarah. "I think the first thing you should do is read through that. It will give you a good idea of our services and our fees, and in addition it will help you understand all the little details that make up the wedding day."

Sarah accepted it with a grateful smile. "Thanks. I know I should have made an appointment."

"That's no problem. I just wish I had more time to talk, but we're planning our big bridal show this Sunday and everything is in sixes and sevens around here."

"Bridal show?"

"It's a wedding extravaganza at the San Francisco Hilton. It runs from noon to four o'clock on Sunday. You and Jeff might want to stop by and take a look. There will be vendors offering every kind of service imaginable, as well as a couple of different fashion shows," she added.

"That sounds wonderful."

"In the meantime read over our brochure, and if you decide you want to work with us you can fill out the contract on the back and then we can set up our first meeting." Kate got to her feet as Sarah walked over to the door.

"Thanks again for letting me interrupt you," Sarah said with a grin.

"No problem," Kate replied, walking out with her to the front office.

Sarah paused at the door. "I may need your help on one more thing, though."

"What's that?"

"Help me convince Barrett that getting married is the right thing to do."

"Sorry, but I've already had that discussion with your brother. You're on your own."

"I was afraid you were going to say that," Sarah replied, waving goodbye as she left.

"What do you mean you've already had that discussion?" Liz asked sharply.

Kate tossed her head nonchalantly. "I told you about our little talk a couple of weeks ago," she replied, pouring herself a cup of coffee.

"Only in the briefest possible way," Liz said. "All I know is that you and Barrett Fox are not fighting anymore, nor are you talking anymore. I also know that he called you three times this week, and you haven't returned any of his calls."

"That just about covers it," Kate replied, nodding her head. "How are you and Rick doing?"

"Don't ask."

"Why not? I thought things were going along great. You actually accepted a drawer and some closet space at his apartment, didn't you?"

Her teasing tone was not lost on Liz, who made a face in response. "I'm beginning to want more than just a drawer, you know."

"Yeah, maybe a cupboard, part of the closet."

"I'm serious," she retorted.

"Good," Kate replied. "I think you deserve more than a drawer, and I'm glad you're beginning to realize that. Maybe we can start planning your wedding soon."

"Hold on, I didn't say marriage. I'm considering living with Rick, that's all."

"Oh."

"Is that all you have to say?" Liz asked impatiently.

"It's your life. If that will make you happy..."

"Well, I haven't told Rick about it, yet. I don't want him to read more into it than there is."

"Why don't you just talk to him about your feelings? Tell him that you want to get closer."

"Oh, Rick and I don't talk about things like that," Liz said. "He's not the kind of guy who talks about feelings and emotions."

Kate smiled. "So make him talk to you. He deserves to know how you feel."

"But I don't know how I feel," Liz wailed. "I thought I did. I thought I knew exactly what I wanted, but now when I see little babies on the streets I want to stop and look at them. I never felt that way before. And yesterday when Jennifer and her fiancé were in here kissing and holding hands, I felt more jealous than annoyed."

Kate laughed at her chagrined expression. "Thank God."

Liz looked at her friend with a knowing smile. "You're doing the same thing I am, you know. Staying away from Barrett Fox because you're afraid of the next step."

"I don't think it's the same thing, at all," Kate protested.

"How are you going to know if Barrett is the right one for you, if you don't give him a chance?"

"I know where he stands on things like this," Kate replied passionately. "It's very cut-and-dried. I'm not foolish enough to think I'm going to change his mind.

A confirmed bachelor is always a challenge. It's kind of romantic to think that you're going to be the one woman to change his mind, that he'll fall so deeply in love that he won't be able to resist you. That's how it happens in all the good books," she said with a small smile.

"You're probably right," Liz conceded. "Usually I'm the one telling you things like that. You must be rubbing off on me."

Kate laughed. "I think there's a little bit more romance in your soul than you realize, and there's probably a little bit more reality in mine. So enough talk about men. How are we looking for the show on Sunday?"

"We're looking good. The video is completed and I think it will be the high point of the show. I've got both Meg and Janice coming in to help on Sunday, so we can concentrate on talking to the brides while they make sure there are enough truffles to go around and that brides get our brochures, and so forth."

"Good. I guess that's it, then. I'll be glad when this weekend is behind us."

"I agree. Are we going to work with Sarah Fox?"

"It looks that way, although I'm really not sure it's a good idea. Barrett is dead set against her getting married, and I certainly don't want to get caught in the middle of that battle. I'm tempted to refuse, but that wouldn't be very nice, would it?"

Liz shook her head. "Business is business. We aren't in a position where we can afford to turn down clients, especially one with money and a doting big brother.''

"Don't remind me—I just got the bills. Let me get them for you," she said with a twinkle in her eyes.

Liz groaned as Kate dumped a pile of mail on her desk. "I'll see you in a couple of days," she complained.

"You better. I can't get through Sunday without you."

Kate was still thinking about their conversation when Liz buzzed through an hour later to let her know that Barrett was on the phone.

"I don't want to talk to him," she said, wishing her stomach wouldn't jump into her throat every time she heard his name.

"He wants to talk to you about Sarah," Liz informed her in a stern tone. "Remember this is our business."

"Oh, all right," Kate said, picking up the phone.

"Kate Marlowe."

"Very efficient," he drawled. "But I'm surprised you came to the phone at all."

"I'm busy, Barrett, is there a point to this call?" She hid the nervousness behind a show of aggression.

"Yes, there is," he said, adopting her formal tone. "Sarah told me she's hired you."

"Not exactly. I gave her a brochure and a contract, but nothing has been finalized."

"I told you that I don't want Sarah to get married, and I don't understand why you're going against my wishes."

She smiled at his tone. He had a tendency to get very formal when he was angry, as if he could freeze someone with icy politeness.

"Sarah is an adult. I can't refuse to work with her just because you don't want her to get married. I think you're being unreasonable. Why don't you get to know her boyfriend, and then make a decision? She told me you've never met the guy."

"You're a fine one to talk," he growled. "You want me to give this kid a chance, but you won't give me a chance."

Kate sighed. This was his real reason for calling, not Sarah.

"I'm not going to give up on you, Kate," he added. "We've both had some time to think over the past few weeks, and I don't know about you but I've missed our daily skirmishes."

"It's better this way," she said, touched by the tender note in his voice.

"Better for who?" he asked in frustration.

"Both of us. I've got to go. I have a lot of work to do."

"Wait, we still need to talk about Sarah. I'll come by tonight and we can discuss it."

"No. I'm going out with Liz tonight. I won't be home until very late."

There was a long silence on his end of the phone as he weighed her words carefully. "So when can we get together?"

"Next week sometime. Maybe the three of us can meet, or the four of us. I'd like to meet Sarah's fiancé, as well."

"Right."

He hung up the phone before she could say anything further, and she looked at the receiver blankly, hoping she had done the right thing.

"Romantic Affairs." Liz answered the phone briskly as she leafed through the stack of bills on her desk.

"This is Barrett Fox."

"Do you want to speak to Kate again?" she asked, smiling to herself. The man certainly got an *A* for effort.

"No, actually I wanted to speak to you," he said smoothly. "I need a favor. I really need to talk to Kate tonight, but she told me that you and she have already made plans, and I was wondering—"

"We have?" Liz interrupted. "That's the first I've heard of it."

"I thought it was probably just an excuse. That's why I need your help. Here's what I want you to do...."

Liz listened to his suggestion with a growing smile, her reluctance fading at the sincerity in his voice.

"What do you think?" he asked, feeling a little like a love-struck teenager.

"I think Kate will probably kill you, not to mention what she'll do to me." She paused. "I'll do it. Just remember to send flowers to my funeral."

He laughed with relief as she agreed to his outlandish suggestion. Lord knows he had never gone to such lengths to get a date, but he had a feeling this woman was worth any amount of effort.

Liz knocked on Kate's door a few minutes later, studying her friend's bent head with a wary eye. She hoped she wasn't making a big mistake, but the paleness in Kate's face convinced her to go ahead. It was time to give cupid a little push. Kate had been moping for the past two weeks.

"Hi," she said, taking a seat in front of the desk. "I have great news for you."

"What's that?" Kate asked, leafing through the Smythe file absentmindedly.

"I'm going to treat you to an evening out tonight."

"What?" she asked in confusion, suddenly realizing Liz was waiting for a response.

"Rick is standing me up," Liz explained. "And I've got two tickets to *Beach Blanket Babylon* and no one to go with."

"The cabaret show? What happened to Rick?"

"He has a business meeting that he says he absolutely cannot get out of, and as you know these tickets are priceless. What do you say—go with me?"

"Sure, I guess so. I don't have anything else planned for tonight."

"Great. Why don't we meet there, because I've got to run to the bank before they close and do some errands. The show starts at eight o'clock, and I'll meet you out front."

Kate glanced down at her watch and saw that it was almost five. "That sounds good. I want to finish up a few things here, and then I can run home and change. Ordinarily I wouldn't dream of going out the Friday before our big show, but I can't believe how organized we are this year."

"I know, it's scary," Liz agreed with a grin. "We must be getting experienced. I'm going to run. See you there."

"Okay." That worked out well. Now her excuse to Barrett wouldn't be a lie. She really was going out with Liz. Not that it mattered, Barrett would never know the difference.

Chapter Ten

Kate arrived at the theater with five minutes to spare, armed with an apology for Liz that included a battery that wouldn't start and a quick call to the Automobile Club. After waiting more than thirty minutes she had canceled the call and taken a cab, hoping she would make it to the theater in time for the show.

There was no sign of Liz as she paid the driver and stepped out of the cab. But then there was no sign of anyone, the show was probably just about to start. She smoothed down the skirt of her rose silk dress and hurried into the lobby.

Most of the crowd had already gone inside, although there were still several people milling around in front of the ticket window. It took her a few moments before she realized Liz was not among them.

Tapping her foot impatiently, she folded her arms and looked around. She couldn't believe Liz was later than she was, and she didn't have the tickets, so there wasn't a thing she could do except wait.

"There you are," a voice said decisively, and she whirled around in dismay. It couldn't be him, not here.

"Hello, Kate."

"Barrett. What are you doing here?"

"I thought I might see the show." He raised his eyebrows curiously. "Are you alone?"

"No. I'm waiting for Liz."

"That's right. You said the two of you were going out tonight. What a coincidence."

"Yes, it is," she said, eyeing his innocent look doubtfully. "What about you? Do you have a date?"

He shook his head in mock sorrow. "No, the only woman I wanted to go out with turned me down flat. So I decided to come alone."

She turned away from him and craned her neck to see if she could see Liz inside the theater, although she doubted that her friend would have gone in without her.

"It doesn't look like Liz is going to make it," he remarked, watching her shift uncomfortably. "The lights are about to go down."

"I guess I'll just wait for her outside. Maybe I'll give her a call," she said, changing her mind. She hurried over to the pay phone in the corner, dialing impatiently. But there was no answer. She turned around to find Barrett standing right next to her.

"Not there?"

"No, she must be on her way."

"Look, I have two tickets and since Liz isn't here yet, why don't we go in and see the show."

"I don't want her to think I left," Kate protested.

"We'll leave a message with the hostess to bring Liz to our table. What do you say?"

"I don't think so." She was irritated by his confidence and was beginning to suspect a setup.

He shook his head impatiently and grabbed her hand. "Come on. Stop thinking of ways to avoid me. It's just a show, for heaven's sake."

"Fine. I'll sit with you," she said, trying to pull her hand away, but he only smiled and held on tightly until they reached their table.

"Just relax and enjoy the show," he advised.

Kate sent him an angry glare, but since there was nothing else to do at the moment she decided to make the best of it. She turned her chair around slightly to face the stage, happy that at least she wouldn't have to look at him. She was trying not to feel anything, but his sexy smile and easy charm were already breaking down her defenses.

The two-hour cabaret was filled with outrageous songs and skits fitting in with the theme of Prom Night. The whole cast of characters from school nerd to the football hero were going to the prom, and the trials and tribulations of adolescent love were highly

entertaining. Kate found herself laughing un-
ashamedly during one sequence and unwittingly
smiled at Barrett as he moved his chair closer to hers.

When the show ended, she was thoroughly relaxed
and didn't protest when he put his arm around her
shoulders as they were leaving.

"That was terrific!" she said, as they left the theater. "I don't know how long it's been since I laughed
like that."

Barrett smiled down at her tenderly. Her sweet face
had haunted him for the last few weeks, and it was
only an enormous amount of work and willpower that
had allowed him to stay away from her. He leaned
down to brush a tendril of hair off her forehead, allowing his lips to rest gently against her soft skin.

Kate looked at him wordlessly, the magic still strong
between them. They were oblivious to the shuffling
crowds and laughter as they stood close together,
touching mentally if not physically. Barrett reached
over to steady her as a rather tipsy group of people
plowed into them, successfully breaking the moment
of tension.

"I guess Liz didn't make it," Kate remarked as they
walked out onto the sidewalk. "I can't imagine what
happened to her."

"It is strange," he agreed, grinning at the knowing
look in her eyes. "I have an idea."

"I'll bet you do."

"I just happen to have dinner reservations at Marcelle's, and I hate to eat alone. Would you join me?"

"Marcelle's? I'm impressed," she said. It was one of the most elegant restaurants in San Francisco, and certainly not one she had much opportunity to frequent.

Pointing to the familiar silver-gray Mercedes parked almost directly in front of the theater, Barrett said gallantly, "Your chariot awaits."

"You didn't have anything to do with my car not starting?" she asked, fixing him with a steely stare.

"Of course not. But since you don't have a car, why don't we go in mine?"

Kate was torn with indecision, wanting to prolong the evening and wanting to run away before she fell more deeply in love with him. She blinked the thought out of her mind. No, she wasn't in love—just infatuated, maybe.

Before she could utter a word of protest, Barrett opened the car door and helped her into her seat.

"How did you wangle this parking spot?" she asked, as he waited for a crowd of pedestrians to move away from the theater.

"One of the benefits of being well-known, I suppose. I also handled the parking manager's divorce about three years ago. He was so grateful he gave me a reserved parking spot."

"I have to admit it's nice." She leaned back against the seat, content to just sit quietly for the moment. It was very pleasant to be taken care of for a change.

Marcelle's was located on the top of Nob Hill, and it took just a few minutes to get there. A parking va-

let helped her out of the car, and **Bar**rett came around
to escort her into the restaurant. After speaking with
the maître d' they were led to a quiet table in the corner.

"Don't tell me you handled his divorce, as well?"
Kate asked, as they sat down at what was clearly one
of the nicest tables in the restaurant.

Barrett laughed. "No, I gave him a big tip."

She shook her head in disbelief, looking around at
the beautifully decorated room with a slight sense of
awe. Everyone was dressed in the height of fashion.
The women were beautiful. The men were handsome.
And in his elegant black suit, Barrett took her breath
away.

She dropped her eyes as he looked up from the wine
list, and was grateful when the waitress arrived, pro-
viding a suitable distraction. She nodded in acquies-
cence as Barrett ordered a bottle of California Pinot
Noir. She wasn't much of a drinker, and she was sure
he would order only the best.

"I should be angry with you," she said when they
were alone again.

"Me?" he asked innocently.

"Yes, I'm quite sure that you and Liz planned this
little rendezvous."

"It's rather romantic, don't you think? We've got
all the right components. We're both dressed up, and
I must say you look absolutely gorgeous in that
dress," he said, his gaze resting on her face. "We saw
a great show, and now we're having a nice dinner with

candlelight and good food, wine to mellow your mood. What more could you want?''

"Nothing. I don't think I could improve on a thing except maybe some soft music and some dancing."

"That comes later," he promised as the waiter brought over their wine. Kate smiled to herself as Barrett declined the ceremonial wine-tasting ritual. He might be rich and powerful, but he was definitely not pompous.

After ordering their dinner they sat back and relaxed, sipping wine and chatting about their days. Kate stopped Barrett as he went to pour her another glass of wine. She had gone through two already, and was feeling light-headed.

"I think I should go easy on the wine," she protested. "I haven't eaten all day."

"Afraid it might loosen you up?" he challenged with a grin.

"No, I'm afraid I might get sick."

He shook his finger at her playfully. "That's not a very romantic thing to say."

"Since when did you learn so much about romance?"

"Since I got interested in a romantic. I know how much women like this kind of stuff. Personally I think any place can be fun if you're with the right person."

"Like a ball game."

"Yeah, like a ball game. We had a good time, didn't we?"

"Yes, it was great," she conceded. But then just about anything was great when Barrett was with her. "How is business going? Lots of marriages breaking up these days?"

He took a sip of his wine before replying. "Unfortunately yes."

"Why unfortunately? That is your business," she pointed out with a wry smile.

"Why don't we talk about your business?" he replied. "Don't you have something big going on this weekend?"

"I'm sure you wouldn't be interested—"

"I'm interested in everything you do—Kate." His tongue caressed her name, his eyes boring into hers with an intensity that made her shiver.

She finally broke their gaze and took another sip of wine, trying to relax. "The bridal fair was created so that brides could meet with all the different vendors they will need to hire at one time and in one place. This can, of course, save them a great deal of time and money."

"Um. But doesn't that cut down on your business? If they can do everything right there, why would they need to hire you?"

"Very good," she said, with admiration at his perceptive comment. "That's what we were worried about at first. But it's interesting; the brides seem to get completely overwhelmed by having all the information right at their fingertips. After seeing all the different florists, photographers, bakers, and so on, they seemed dazed, and when they get to our booth, it's like a light goes on in their head. They suddenly realize they don't have to deal with everything by themselves, they can just hire Romantic Affairs, and we'll do the dealing for them."

Barrett chuckled at her enthusiasm. "I bet that's your sales pitch."

"What do you think? Would you buy it?"

"Sounds great to me. But can they afford you? I'm sure your services don't come cheap."

"We have different prices for different services. A bride can buy all or some of our services. It's up to her and her budget. Of course, we also believe that we will save her money in the long run, because we know who to hire and who offers the most for the money."

He tapped his long, tapered fingers on the table thoughtfully. "You're a smart businesswoman, sweetheart. I'm a little surprised."

Kate looked at him in disgust. "I hope you're not going to tell me a woman should be in the home and not in the business world."

He laughed at her indignant expression. "I wouldn't think of it. I've often worked with female attorneys and have found them to be just as good as their male counterparts. But I have to tell you that most of the businesswomen I know are a lot harder than you, very sharp, and ruthless would be a good description. But you—" he reached out to clasp her hand across the table, "you are sweet and sensitive and very caring."

His voice dropped down to a whisper and Kate had to lean closer to hear him.

She looked at him with her heart in her eyes, touched by his description. He was much more sensitive than she had first thought. He was much more of a man than she had realized.

"Barrett," she began, only to be interrupted by the arrival of their dinner. She sat back in her seat, her face a portrait of conflicting emotions. It didn't help that Barrett was staring at her with an intensity that made her feel that he was reading her mind. She averted her gaze, smiling at the waiter as he served her a large portion of prime rib.

"What were you going to say?" Barrett asked quietly. "I don't remember," she lied, picking up her fork. "This looks delicious. I'm starving."

He shook his head as she ignored his questioning eyes. Then a soft smile curved his lips as he remembered the flash of desire he had seen in her eyes. There would be time to talk later. He would make sure of that.

Perhaps it was the wine, or maybe it was just the intoxicating feeling she had when she was with Barrett, but Kate could remember little of what she ate. She knew they exchanged casual conversation over the meal, but she couldn't remember what it was about. The only thing that stood out in her mind was Barrett looking at her tenderly, lovingly.

They sat quietly as the waitress cleared away the plates and brought them their check. Kate felt at a loss for words. There was so much she wanted to say and so much she couldn't say. Barrett was also quiet, and aside from casting her strange, enigmatic looks, he seemed caught up in his own thoughts, as well. She sighed in relief when they finally left the intimate atmosphere of the restaurant and headed for home.

He drove her back to her apartment quickly, and as they neared her street she felt a rush of disappointment that the evening was ending so soon. This would have to be their last evening together, if she wanted to hang on to her heart.

Having made her silent promise Kate did not demur when he offered to walk her to her apartment, nor did she say a word when he followed her inside on the pretext of checking things over. One kiss, she told herself. One kiss to remember him by. Surely she could handle that.

"Everything okay?" she asked, as he poked his head into the bedroom.

"Um, I'm not sure yet." He walked over to join her with a serious look on his face. Then he deliberately placed his hands on her waist and pulled her against him. With his breath fanning her cheek, he leaned over and placed a kiss behind her left ear. The moist warmth of his mouth made her shiver and she instinctively turned her lips toward him, welcoming his mouth with a hunger of her own.

His cheek felt rough against her soft skin, as his mouth roamed over her face, placing kisses on her eyes, the tip of her nose and coming to rest on the side of her neck.

"I want to make love to you, Kate," he whispered. "I want to undress you and hold your warm, soft body in my arms. I want to kiss you here and here," and he placed a kiss on the tiny pulse throbbing wildly in her throat and then down along the soft swell of her breasts where her neckline revealed a tantalizing portion of soft flesh. "You are so sweet, so delicious."

Kate felt herself drowning as his seductive tone enveloped her and his fingers stroked her neck sensuously. The touch of his lips sent shock waves through her body, conscious thought fleeing as her emotions took over.

She didn't protest when she felt the flutter of the zip down her back. The desire to feel his hands on her skin was too strong to be denied and she let out a soft sigh as he stroked her back, his fingers lingering at her waist before curving around to cup her breasts.

"We should stop," she muttered, her roaming hands belying her words. She had unconsciously undone the buttons on his shirt and her hand slipped inside to caress his warm chest, the tiny tuft of hair at the base of his neck.

"I don't want to stop," he replied, gazing into her eyes. "I want you to keep on touching me." He placed his hand over hers, holding it to his chest.

It was only a split second that they stood there motionless, but it was enough time for Kate to realize they were approaching the point of no return. There were still too many unanswered questions. Reluctantly she pulled away.

"I don't think we should do this," she said. "We should talk."

"We will, later," he promised.

She took a step back. Her blue eyes were bright with passion, her lips soft and full from his touch, and as he stared at her he thought she was the most beautiful woman he had ever known and possibly the most vulnerable. He could hurt her so easily. The realization shocked him into silence.

"Please go," she whispered, before her defenses completely crumbled.

He shook his head, his eyes darkening with worry. She was so pale, all of a sudden. "I'm sorry if I rushed things. I thought we were feeling the same way."

"No."

"Kate, there is something going on between us."

"No. No, there's not."

"God, you're a stubborn woman," he complained. "But so am I. I fight for things I want. I thought you did, too."

"I do." She paused, drumming up her courage. "I just don't want you."

"Liar," he snapped. "You weren't faking your response just now. You wanted to make love every bit as much as I did."

"There's an attraction. I admit it," she said with growing annoyance. "But I'm not interested in a casual affair."

"Who said it was going to be casual?"

"Don't play games. We know each other well enough not to pretend things that we don't feel. You know what I want out of life, Barrett. I haven't made any secret of my desire for a long-lasting love that leads to marriage. I just won't settle for anything else. I can't. Please, try and understand."

He stared at her for a long moment. "I do understand. I just don't know what to do about it. Because I don't think I can let you go."

"You have to. We both have to just try and be friends, business acquaintances, neighbors. I like talking with you, sharing things. I don't want to lose you entirely," she said wistfully.

He shook his head. "I don't think you have to worry about that. Good night, Kate."

"Good night," she whispered into the air as he shut the door behind him. Closing her eyes, she let herself remember, just for a moment.

"Please feel free to give me a call when you're ready to start planning your wedding," Kate said cheerfully, handing a young lady and her mother a business card. She took a quick look around their booth. Liz was engaged in conversation with another couple and Meg was running the video for an interested group of spectators. Thankful for a break in the action, she sat down for a moment and took a deep breath.

The bridal show was a huge success, and she and Liz had been on their feet for the past five hours. Two hours of setup and three hours of patient smiling were exhausting, and she was beginning to feel a little wilted. More than eight hundred prospective brides had come through the show since it opened at noon, and with an hour and a half to go it looked like they might break one thousand this year, an enormous success by anyone's standards.

Their booth had drawn quite a bit of attention, thanks to the innovative videotape and a large supply of chocolate truffles. Liz had also set up a computer program whereby she would sit down with a bride and do budget analysis based on the number of guests expected, the size of the wedding party and the overall style. Within ten minutes she could come up with a generalized budget sample. If the bride was interested in taking it further, Liz offered her an office consultation for a flat fifty-dollar fee. It was a marketing strategy that seemed to be pulling in a lot of potential clients.

"It looks like things are winding down," Liz groaned, taking a seat next to Kate. "One more hour to go."

"Thank God," Kate said fervently. Not only had the day been exhausting, she was still suffering from two nights of very little sleep. She hadn't heard from Barrett since Friday night, and despite her best intentions she couldn't stop thinking about him.

"Oh, look," Liz exclaimed, pointing toward the fashion-show area. "Isn't that Sarah Fox?"

"Yes, I think so." She craned her neck hoping to catch a glimpse of Barrett's sister. For a frightening moment she thought he might be with her, but then she saw a sandy-haired young man put a casual arm around her waist as they looked at a photography book. "That must be her fiancé."

"They make a nice couple," Liz remarked. "But then everyone looks pretty good at their age."

Kate laughed at her cynical remark. "You don't look so bad yourself, and Rick is certainly no slouch."

"That's true," she admitted, studying Kate with a worried expression. "I hope you're not angry with me about Friday night."

"You mean the way you set me up with Barrett Fox," Kate drawled, refusing to let her off the hook too lightly. "That wasn't a nice thing to do."

"I'm sorry, I just felt bad for the guy. He seemed so desperate to see you. I thought it was my romantic duty to give you two a little help."

"Since when have you done anything for romance?" Kate asked in exasperation. "You certainly picked a fine time to start."

"You're rubbing off on me," Liz grumbled, getting to her feet as another group of brides approached. "I hope it wasn't a horrible evening for you."

"It was okay."

"Just okay?" she queried, putting on her professional face as she waited for the next group.

"It was nice," Kate replied. "Very nice. But that's it. No more dates, no more favors for so-called desperate men. Okay?"

"You got it," Liz said, as she walked over to answer someone's questions.

"Miss Marlowe, hello," Sarah called, dragging her young man by the arm. "I was hoping we would see you. Wow! your booth is fantastic."

"Great truffles," Jeff adding, stuffing one of the chocolates into his mouth.

"This is Jeff Chandler, my fiancé," Sarah said with a grin. "I promised him food if he would come with me."

"Men aren't too keen on these things," Kate conceded.

"I just can't believe everything there is to do to plan a wedding," Sarah continued. "I'm glad you're going to be helping us. I wouldn't want to handle all of this on my own. I wish my mother were still around," she said wistfully, forcing away her sadness with a bright smile. "But I'm sure we can handle everything."

Kate had been debating whether or not to handle Sarah's wedding, but the sad mention of her mother pushed aside her own doubts and insecurities. Sarah needed a friend right now, and she didn't want to disappoint her, even if it meant seeing Barrett more than she wanted to.

"Have you talked things over with your brother?" she inquired.

"Yes, he's still adamant about my not getting married," Sarah replied. "But I'm working on him. I don't need his approval, of course, but I would like it. Jeff's parents aren't thrilled, either. They want him to finish medical school first."

Kate smiled compassionately at them. "Sometimes once the initial shock wears off, people change their minds."

"I hope you're right," Sarah said fervently. "That's why I've invited Jeff and Barrett over to dinner Wednesday night. I want Barrett to get to know Jeff so he can see how happy we're going to be together."

"That sounds like a good idea."

"Well, keep your fingers crossed. I guess we should hold off on our meeting until after Wednesday, unless," she snapped her fingers, "unless you could come, too, and then we could discuss everything at once."

Kate looked at her in dismay. "I don't think that would be a good idea, Sarah. This is a family matter."

"It would be perfect. You could act as a buffer, an objective third party, and I know Barrett respects your opinion."

Kate shook her head. "No, I don't think so."

Sarah paused as a group of young women stopped at the booth. "Promise me you'll think about it. I'll talk to you tomorrow."

"What was that all about?" Liz asked as Sarah walked away.

"She wants me to come to dinner and help convince Barrett that getting married is a good idea."

"What did you say?"

"I tried to say no, but she's very much like her brother in that regard."

"Doesn't take no for an answer."

"Right. I don't know what to do. What do you think?"

"Maybe you should back out of this one," Liz suggested. "I'm beginning to think you were right to stay away from Barrett." She paused as the booth cleared out leaving them alone for the moment. "I'm worried about you. You seem different today. One minute you're happy and smiling, and the next minute you look like you lost your best friend."

Kate sighed, pausing for a moment as a young woman stopped in front of their display. "Can I help you?"

"No, thanks," the girl replied. "We've already got everything taken care of."

"Well?" Liz prodded when they were alone again.

Kate smiled wanly. "I'm very confused about what I want and don't want. Barrett and I had a wonderful time Friday night. We talked and laughed and then when we got to my place, we..." Her voice faltered as her emotions overwhelmed her.

"What happened? Did he make a pass?"

"In a way, yes, but I was a willing participant. He's too attractive, too smooth. He makes me forget what I want."

"Sounds like you don't trust him."

"I'm afraid to."

"I think you should give him a chance. Maybe you're wrong about him."

"I doubt that," Kate retorted. "Anyway I can handle it."

"You can handle seeing him every day and planning his sister's wedding?"

"I don't have any other choice," Kate replied. "He's not going to move because of me, and I feel sorry for Sarah. She needs someone to help her. Barrett certainly isn't going to do anything for her, not in this matter. And I like her."

Liz shook her head. "You should back out right now, Kate. You're already in love with the guy. What's going to happen if you have to keep seeing him, maybe with other women?"

"I'll deal with it," Kate replied. She wished she felt as confident as she sounded.

Chapter Eleven

It was late afternoon on Wednesday, and Kate still hadn't decided whether or not she was going to go to dinner at Sarah's. She had tried to beg off several times, but Sarah's anxious pleas were beginning to get to her. An hour ago she had given her a definite maybe, which certainly wasn't the most professional way to behave, but then this situation was a little more complicated than Sarah realized.

For one thing she hadn't seen or spoken to Barrett since he had walked out of her apartment Friday night. She didn't think she could handle seeing him for the first time in front of two other people. But then again she hated to disappoint Sarah just because she and Barrett were having personal problems.

She threw her pencil down on the desk in frustration, swearing softly as her elbow knocked over a stack of papers on one side. It was not her day. It was definitely not her day. As she bent over to pick them up, a familiar baritone voice called her name, and she cracked her head against the corner of the desk as she stared angrily at Barrett.

"You scared me to death," she accused, rubbing one side of her head with her hand.

"Sorry, I didn't see you at first." He sat down in front of her desk and crossed his legs casually, fixing her with an intense stare. "I told you I don't give up easily. That's why I'm here. I've been doing a lot of thinking about the two of us. Actually I've come to a rather startling realization."

"What's that?"

"I think that I might be in love with you," he said pragmatically.

Her mouth dropped open at his words. "You think you might be," she repeated. "Doesn't sound like you're very sure of your feelings."

"I'm still trying to figure them out," he admitted. He leaned forward, an intent look on his face. "But what I really want to know is how you feel about me?"

"I don't think this is the time or the place to be discussing our feelings," she said.

"I know it's not romantic, not in the slightest."

"That's not what I meant."

"Then tell me how you feel. Is it so difficult to be honest with me?"

"I care about you," she started.

"Care is a Milquetoast word. Tell me how you really feel."

"I like you."

He snorted in disgust. "Like is a—"

"Stop interrupting me," she said angrily. "I'll pick my own words."

"I just want the truth. If you hate me, say so. If you love me, let me hear the words."

There was a silent plea in his eyes that told her how important her answer was. But he was backing her into a corner, and she didn't like that. "Okay, Barrett. I love you, did you hear me? I love you. There I said it, now please go."

He smiled at her flushed face with a tenderness that stilled any further protests. "Do you have to sound so angry when you say it?"

"What do you expect? You asked me for an answer, I gave you one. I don't want to be in love with you. There are times, like right now, when I don't even like you very much. But there's no accounting for emotions." She paused. "I'm afraid I have some very strong ones for you," she added.

"Good. Because I feel the same way. We can't stop pushing this aside. What we have together is too important to let just drift away."

"But Barrett—"

"I know, you want commitment. I don't know if I can give you one. I'm trying to be honest with you. My marriage was a disaster, a painful, horrible experience. I don't know if I can go through all that again.''

"It doesn't have to be that way," she argued. "We might be different together than you and Caroline. Maybe your love wasn't strong enough.''

"I'm sure it wasn't," he agreed. "I guess I'm afraid.''

She sighed. "I am, too. I know you don't think a piece of paper is important, but it is to me. I need that security.''

"Just trust me, Kate. I don't ever want to hurt you," he said solemnly. "I would gladly give you my own personal vows, isn't that enough?''

She thought about his words for a long moment. The proposition was a tempting one, to see Barrett every day, to share their lives together. But what would happen to her if he did walk away? She had seen it happen to her mother so many times. Men who professed undying love suddenly disappeared without a moment's notice. How could she trust him not to do the same thing?

No, it was better to break things off now, before it was too late. Why couldn't he see that? Why did he have to keep pressuring her?

"No," she said finally. "I don't think I can live that way.''

His smile faded as he studied her pale face. There was a stubborn light in her eyes that he was beginning to recognize only too well. He supposed he had known all along that she wasn't going to just give up on her ideals. She wasn't that kind of woman. But he couldn't walk out of her life. He wasn't that big a fool.

She watched him stalk restlessly around the office, his mind wrestling with their problem. It would be so easy to give in, just enjoy life for the moment. He was a wonderful, loving man. He would be good to her, she knew that instinctively. But something held her back.

"Why don't you think about it?" he suggested, finally coming to a stop at the side of her desk. "I don't want to leave things on a bad note. Friends?"

She stared at him for a long moment, a tiny smile curving her lips as she remembered their meeting on the Hunts' balcony when she had asked him if they could be friends. It seemed like a lifetime ago.

"What do you say?" he prodded gently.

She should say no, but his lazy smile was her weakness. She couldn't bear the thought of never seeing him again. "Okay, friends."

"Good." He stood up with a satisfied grin. "But we still have a small problem, my sister and her crazy wedding plans."

Kate nodded her head, relaxing as he changed the subject. "Yes, she did invite me to dinner tonight, but to be honest I still haven't decided whether or not to go. Perhaps I should step back right now."

"No, Sarah needs your help and despite my arguments she seems determined to go through with this. That's why I agreed to meet Jeff tonight. It will be my last chance at talking them out of this potential mess."

"I don't think I'd refer to it in those terms," she said dryly.

"I'll be tactful," he promised, his face darkening into a frown. "I just hope he has the right answers to my questions."

"Now you sound like an attorney. Are you going to put him on the witness stand?"

"I'd like to," he said. "But I'm sure my sister wouldn't allow it, and I have a feeling you're not going to be much help on my side."

"I'm strictly neutral," she replied. "But at the moment, I'm also busy. I have an appointment in fifteen minutes, so—"

"I'm going. I'll pick you up at seven."

"Why don't I just meet you there?" she protested. "Doesn't she live down in the Sunset District?"

"Yes, she moved there last year. I guess that was the beginning of her independence. It's a hole-in-the-wall compared to the huge house she was living in, but nothing mattered to her except being on her own."

Kate grinned at his frustrated expression. "It's tough being a parent, isn't it? You have to learn when to let go."

"Of children, yes, and even sisters, but not the woman I want."

Kate flushed as she stared into his dark, compelling eyes. "I thought we agreed to drop the subject," she said, averting her gaze.

There was a long, brittle silence.

"I'll pick you up at seven."

"It's not necessary. I can go on my own." She repeated her protest halfheartedly.

"No way. I want to make sure you come." He paused as Liz walked into the office with a curious smile on her face. "Hello."

"Hello," she replied. "Are the two of you actually having a civil conversation?"

"Just barely," Kate remarked dryly.

"That's an improvement, anyway," she replied, smiling at Barrett. "Samantha Davis is here, Kate."

"I'll see you tonight," Barrett added, strolling leisurely out the door.

"He'll see you tonight?" Liz echoed.

"Sarah's wedding meeting," Kate explained. "You know she's been pressuring me to go. Since Barrett and I have reached an understanding, I don't see any reason why I shouldn't go."

"What understanding?"

"Liz, I have an appointment."

"Just give me the highlights—Samantha is looking at the photograph albums, anyway. What happened?"

"We're going to be friends, that's all."

"Sure. Whatever you say. So tell me why do you look a little more cheerful than you did an hour ago?"

Kate laughed in exasperation. "I don't know why I don't feel bad. I should. There is no hope of a permanent relationship here. But he did admit that he cared about me. It helps."

Liz shook her head. "Somehow I don't think that's going to console you in the long, lonely days ahead. I think you and Barrett are meant to be together. Maybe you should consider compromising."

"You mean sleep with him, move in with him? But then I would be making all the compromises," she protested.

"You know, Kate, there's something I've come to learn from my relationship with Rick, and that's that you can't keep score. I always want everything to be fair. I do something for him, he does something for me. But it doesn't work that way. Sometimes I feel like I've spent months worrying about him, helping him with his job, and no return for me. But then the pendulum swings back the other way, and I'm the one who needs his help, and you know what—he's there for me. I know I grumble all the time about him. But there are times when I think I would die if he wasn't around." She paused. "Maybe you better think about what you want more, your pride, a marriage license, or the man you love." She walked to the door. "I'll send Samantha in."

Liz's words haunted her for the rest of the day, and she was still thinking about their conversation as she searched for something suitable to wear to dinner.

She wasted twenty minutes fruitlessly trying on one outfit after another. Annoyed with herself for caring so much, she finally settled for a winter-white lambswool sweater dress that hugged her curves and made a striking contrast with her dark hair. She decided to leave her hair long since it was an informal evening, but she pulled the sides back with two silver combs, not realizing how much the hairstyle accentuated her beautiful bone structure. Even with all her nervous preparations, she was still ready fifteen minutes early.

Her stomach was filled with butterflies as she thought ahead to an evening in Barrett's company. Maybe Liz was right, and she was kidding herself thinking that she could put him out of her life forever. The one simple promise she had made to herself to keep things platonic flew out of her mind every time he looked at her, smiled at her, touched her. Her cheeks flushed as the doorbell rang.

Just be cool, she told herself sharply, taking a moment to smooth down her dress and regain her composure. She forced a polite smile on her face and opened the door.

"Hi."

"Hi." Desire ripped through his brown eyes, quickly hidden by his long black lashes. "Are you ready?"

"Yes." She grabbed her purse and coat off the table before he could come inside. It was safer that way. "Let's go."

She tried not to look at him as they walked down to his car. But her loving eyes had already taken in every detail from his open-necked blue knit shirt to the slim-fitting gray trousers. There wasn't an ounce of fat on his long, lean body, and she loved the way he moved with silent power, quietly, effortlessly.

He opened the car door for her, politely waiting for her to take a seat before going around to his side. Kate smiled as he slid into the car, trying to break the sudden feeling of tension that assailed her. The last thing she wanted to do was ruin Sarah's evening by exchanging stilted conversation with Barrett.

"I hope you're not too hungry," Barrett said casually as they sped across the city.

She looked at him in surprise. "I thought Sarah was cooking dinner."

"She is. But she's not the greatest cook in the world. She tends to get impatient, and instead of following directions she just throws everything together."

"I'm sure it will be fine."

"Don't be so sure, she almost poisoned me once," he said, his face brightening as he thought of something. "Maybe her cooking will scare this guy away."

Kate shook her head in disgust. "You're terrible, and I don't think comments like that are going to help you in this situation."

"You're right. Just promise me one thing, Kate."

"What?"

"Don't start talking hearts-and-flowers until we have a chance to see if this guy is worth anything."

She sent him a frown. "Believe me, the last thing I want to do is get in the middle of this situation."

* * *

Famous last words, Kate thought idly as she sat between a shouting Barrett and a disgusted Sarah. Dinner was an abysmal failure. Sarah's chicken cordon bleu looked more like a melted cheese mess and the rice was soggier than the cheese. Even Jeff looked a little discouraged by the meal.

She glanced across the table at the sandy-haired young man. He was a quiet man, attractive in a boyish way, and seemed to be pretty nice. Not that he'd had much of an opportunity to speak; Barrett and Sarah had been at each other's throats since they first arrived.

"What do you think, Kate?" Barrett asked sharply.

"Yes, what do you think?" Sarah echoed.

Kate looked from one to the other with a blank expression on her face. "Could you repeat the question?"

Barrett sighed in frustration. "I just told Sarah that planning a wedding in three months is nearly impossible."

Kate nodded, feeling on fairly safe ground. "That's true," she agreed. "I did mention that before, not that it can't be done," she amended, trying to take the hurt look off Sarah's face. "What I'm saying is—"

"What are you saying?" Barrett asked impatiently.

She threw up her hands in disgust. "Look, I am not going to take a side here. I'm a wedding consultant, not a marriage counselor or a referee. The answer is yes; you can plan a wedding in three months, but I daresay not the kind of wedding that you said you wanted, Sarah. If you really want to do it right, with all the trimmings, you should give yourself at least six months. Many of the places you would interested in booking are filled up a year in advance.''

She got to her feet. "Now Jeff and I are going to walk down to the corner and pick up a pizza while you and your sister decide what you want to do.''

Barrett took one look at her angry face and reached into his pocket for his wallet. "Here's some money,'' he said, a gleam of admiration in his eyes. "Go easy on the onions.''

"I hope you don't mind going with me,'' she said to Jeff, who had jumped to his feet at the suggestion.

"Not at all,'' he said with obvious relief. "Okay, honey?'' He turned to Sarah with a concerned look.

"You go on,'' she replied. "I'll try not to kill him before you get back.''

"Maybe I should go with you,'' Barrett said hastily.

Kate shook her head. "No way. You two stay here and thrash this thing out.'' She followed Jeff out the door.

They spent the next half hour waiting for their pizza and chatting about the upcoming wedding. Kate found him to be a very serious, sensitive young man who was truly in love. She didn't think Barrett stood a chance.

Brother and sister were sitting docilely on the couch when they returned to the apartment. Kate looked at them both warily before setting the pizza down on the kitchen table.

Barrett started to chuckle at her nervous expression, and Sarah joined in, until both Jeff and Kate were staring at them uncertainly.

"Don't look so worried," Barrett said finally. "We've had a chance to talk, thanks to you." He sent Kate a loving smile. "We've both made a few compromises."

Kate looked at them expectantly. "Well?"

Sarah smiled. "If it's all right with Jeff, I've agreed to give us nine months to plan the wedding. Around Christmas would be nice."

"Winter weddings can be very beautiful," Kate agreed.

"And I'm going to spend more time getting to know my future brother-in-law," Barrett said quietly. He extended a hand to the younger man. "If that's okay with you?"

Jeff nodded, a big smile lighting up his face. "This is great. Let's eat." He opened the pizza box and passed it around the table.

"You got onions," Barrett said, for Kate's ears alone.

"Don't you like them?" she asked innocently, munching on her piece of pizza.

"Not when I'm out on a date."

"It's a good thing this isn't a date."

"What are you two being so secretive about?" Sarah asked curiously.

"I was whispering sweet nothings into her ear," Barrett said, rubbing the back of her neck with his fingers.

Kate sent him a dark look, but ignored his teasing comment. She managed to change the subject and move away from his caressing fingers all at the same time. Conversation drifted into more neutral channels with the only controversy centering around the Dodgers and the Giants. Apparently Jeff was also a baseball fanatic, and Sarah and Kate exchanged a long, pointed look as the two men began to bond over baseball.

She knew Barrett was going to give in, and watching the three of them together left a bittersweet taste in her mouth. It was heaven to be with them, pretending to share in their sense of family. She longed to hear the same love in Barrett's voice when he spoke to her as when he spoke to Sarah. She wanted to be the recipient of his gentle, caring smile. And she was to a certain extent, but in her mind nothing could compare to the commitment of marriage, the ties of a family. If Barrett didn't love her enough to marry, then he wasn't the right man for her.

In her head, she knew she was right to break the tenuous link between them, but in her heart she was afraid she was making a terrible mistake.

Chapter Twelve

Do you think this is going to work?'' Liz cried as the wind blew her words away.

''I hope so,'' Kate said, trying to wedge one of the poles of the tent more deeply into the soil. ''Damn. Wouldn't you know it would have to rain on the only outdoor wedding we have planned for the next three months.''

Liz pushed the sandbag around the bottom part of the pole, stabilizing the tent. They had spent the last hour trying to cover the patio area at the Blossom Hill Mansion from an unexpected spring shower. The wedding party was due to arrive within ten minutes and the caterers were still waiting impatiently to set up the tables.

"I think it will be all right," Liz said firmly, taking another look at the structure. "That's what these tents are for, to keep out the rain."

"I know, but I always worry the darn thing is going to come toppling down on someone's head and after a huge lawsuit, Romantic Affairs will become a distant memory."

"Thanks for the vote of confidence," Liz said sarcastically. "Come on, let's help the caterers get going. They're going to be here in just a few minutes."

Two hours later the party was in full swing. The sun had broken through the clouds and most of the party had moved out from under the tent onto the uncovered part of the patio. The only thing left to do was throw the bouquet and garter and cut the cake. Then they could call it a day.

"Tired?" Liz asked quietly.

Kate nodded her head. "I'm looking forward to soaking in a hot tub. This has been quite a weekend."

"No kidding. I don't think we should schedule a Friday-night wedding followed by two on Saturday, not unless we have at least two more hands to help out."

"Agreed," Kate said with a smile.

"At least we get a break next weekend, not one wedding scheduled. It's hard to believe, a quiet weekend in April."

"I know, I'm looking forward to it. This week has been exhausting."

"You do look tired," Liz agreed. "Why don't you go on home, I can finish up here."

Kate's eyes brightened at the thought of some blessed solitude. "I might just take you up on that. I'd love to go home, put on my jeans, sit in front of the television and watch all of those horrible Saturday-evening shows."

"Sounds great. Unfortunately Rick and I are going to a party tonight."

"Maybe you should go home, then," Kate suggested with a considerate smile.

"No, it's no big deal. Go on, get out of here." She gave her a gentle push. "And don't forget to call Barrett. He's been trying to reach you for days."

"I know, but I really just want to stay away from the man."

"Why? So you can continue being unhappy? Face it, Kate, the light's gone out of your life since you said goodbye to him last week."

"It's temporary."

"You hope," Liz called as Kate hastily made her exit.

The rest of the weekend passed in a showery rain that did little to improve her flagging spirits. By Monday she was ready to go back to work, eager to bury herself once again in the business that was becoming her whole life.

She tried to tell herself that owning Romantic Affairs was enough for now, that she didn't need love or a special man in her life to make her happy. But the hectic chaos of the following week did nothing to alleviate the empty feeling in her heart.

She passed Barrett a few times in the hallway, shared a few stolen moments at the delicatessen down the street, but other than that they had little contact with each other. She didn't know whether to feel relieved or disappointed. She was afraid he had lost interest and at the same time she hoped he had. She was a mass of emotions, one spilling into the other, until she didn't know if she was smiling through her tears or crying through her laughter. It was time to come to terms with the situation.

Escape. It was the only answer. A weekend with no weddings seemed fatefully appropriate. She needed time to think. And there was only one place on earth she wanted to go, home.

San Francisco was completely fogged in when she left for Mendocino shortly after eight o'clock on Saturday morning. But within minutes she was over the Golden Gate Bridge and on the open highway, heading into the distant sunshine. It had been a long time since she had made the long drive home, and her Honda whizzed along merrily, as if it was also grateful for a chance to blow off some steam.

By the time she pulled into Mendocino, it was just after noon, and the town square was crowded with visitors. She drove through the downtown area reminiscing at the sight of the familiar storefronts and restaurants. She was glad to see that progress had made only a small dent in her hometown. She waited anxiously at the last stoplight out of town, suddenly eager to get home.

Once back on the highway it took another fifteen minutes to reach her grandparents' house, which was located on a bluff overlooking the Pacific Ocean. A narrow, winding road led up to the house, which was set a few miles away from the nearest neighbor. Of simple design, it was a cozy three-bedroom home surrounded by redwood trees and wildflowers.

A welcoming brass placard, rusted from the sea air, sat atop their porch railing, and brought a drop of moisture to her eyes as she read the familiar greeting, "Welcome to our tiny slice of paradise." She fit her key into the lock and took a deep breath of the musty air. The house was looked after by one of the neighbors and it still looked warm and homey.

Dropping her overnight bag inside the door, she looked around and smiled. Her grandmother's knick-knacks were still lovingly placed around the room, and the mantel was covered with photos from her childhood.

Moving further into the house, the patio doors beckoned her. She walked out onto the redwood deck that wound around the entire back of the house offering a spectacular view of the ocean below. Leaning against the railing, she drank in the view. The waves were high and crashing against the rocks below, and she could feel salty moisture on her face as she leaned over the side.

Tossing her long hair in the wind, she took several deep breaths of the fresh air and thought back to all the times she had brought her troubles out onto this deck, hoping the wind and sea could blow them away.

The faint sound of children laughing drifted through the air, and Kate suddenly smiled, a feeling of lightness taking over her body. During the past few years she had come to remember her home as a place of pain and unhappiness. In her memories she saw everything through a cold, dreary fog. But now, at this moment, she began to remember the good times. The laughing, carefree days spent hiking in the nearby hills, building castles in the sand and wading out into the bitterly cold Pacific Ocean.

She stood at the railing for nearly half an hour, the salt spray mingling with the cleansing tears of healing. She was right. It had been time to come home, time to remember and then to forget. Her father's desertion, the lies about her birth, her mother's ambivalent love had haunted her for too long. It was time to take charge of the future instead of remaining a victim of the past.

She still didn't know if Barrett would be a part of that future, for there were some things that she couldn't let go of, and one was her desire for a lifelong commitment.

Barrett stood outside their office building, staring up at the upstairs window for perhaps the hundredth time. Tapping his fingers indecisively on the railing, he turned his back on the building and gazed unseeing down the street. It had been three long weeks since he and Kate had parted, three weeks of intense soul-searching and no answers.

"Perhaps a flower would help," a gruff voice said, interrupting his thoughts. He turned around to see Mr. Ramoni holding out a bouquet of spring flowers.

"Unfortunately I don't think a flower will do it," he said ironically.

Mr. Ramoni nodded back understandingly. "Sometimes it takes more than a flower to win a lady's heart. It took me a long time to learn that. In fact if it wasn't for Miss Marlowe I'd be wearing the same sad expression you've got on your face."

"Ah yes, her romantic remedies," Barrett said with a grin. Suddenly he snapped his fingers. "That's it, romance. I think you've just solved my problem."

"She likes white roses," Mr. Ramoni said slyly.

Barrett laughed. "Better make it a dozen. I need all the help I can get."

Kate looked up in surprise as Mr. Ramoni placed a bouquet of roses on her desk.

"For you," he said with a big grin that lit up his face.

Liz smiled knowingly. "I wonder who they're from."

Kate tossed her head casually. "Is there a card?" she asked, her heart pounding against her chest.

"No card. Secret admirer," he replied, walking out of the office with a chuckle.

"Secret admirer, huh?" Liz remarked. "I wonder who that could be?"

"I haven't the faintest idea." Then, glancing at the clock, she said, "Good grief, I'm supposed to be downtown right now."

Liz smiled as Kate grabbed her briefcase and dashed out the door. She picked up the flowers and shook her head in relief. Thank God, someone was finally coming to his senses.

The beautiful bouquet of roses lingered in Kate's mind as she worked through a two-hour meeting with the Hilton Hotel, and she was still thinking about them when she walked wearily up the stairs to her office just after seven that evening. She was bone-tired, having buried herself in work for the past three weeks, trying to think about anything but Barrett. Not that it took a dozen roses to remind her. He hadn't been out of her thoughts for one moment.

She sat down at her desk with a groan and began unloading her briefcase. She was still debating whether or not to put in another hour or just go home and collapse when the downstairs doorbell rang. Deciding it would be unwise just to buzz someone in at this late hour, she hurried down the stairs, expecting to see one of her nervous brides on the doorstep, but instead she found two men dressed in waiters' uniforms, each holding a large silver tray.

"What is all this?" she asked in surprise.

"Kate Marlowe? Romantic Affairs?" one of the men asked, glancing down at a card in his hand.

"Yes," she said still mystified by the delicious aroma spreading through the hallway.

"Then this is for you. Would you mind letting us in before everything gets cold?"

"But I don't understand. I didn't order anything."

"I think we have a note that explains everything," the other waiter interrupted. "It's here somewhere. Would you mind if we came in and set this stuff down?"

Kate reluctantly opened the door and led them upstairs to her office. Her eyes widened in disbelief as they pulled the lids off the trays revealing an elegant meal of Cornish game hens surrounded by wild rice, a plate of steaming vegetables, hot rolls and whipped butter, strawberry cheesecake, a pitcher of coffee and a bottle of extremely expensive white wine.

"Here's the note we promised you," the young man said, whipping out an envelope with an amused grin. "He said not to give it to you until we had unloaded everything."

"Thank you," Kate said, taking the envelope in one hand. "How much do I owe you?"

"Nothing. He took care of the tip and everything." He turned to walk out the door. "Just leave the trays here. Someone will pick them up in the morning."

Kate looked down at her meal in amazement and then at the unopened card in her hand. It didn't take a genius to know that Barrett had sent this meal. She just couldn't figure out why. It was such a romantic gesture and totally out of character.

She unfolded the note slowly, almost frightened of what she would read.

Dear Kate,
They say the way to a man's heart is through his
stomach. I hope that works for a certain blue-
eyed beauty, as well.

                                        Barrett.

Her mouth curved into a smile as she looked down
at the note and then down at her meal. The man was
getting tough. He was going after her Achilles' heel
now, food. Still, it was going to take more than a
Cornish game hen to change her mind.

The meal was delicious, everything was perfect except for one thing, no Barrett. The romantic gesture
seemed strangely hollow without his scoffing remarks, lazy smile and sexy brown eyes. She sat back
in her chair and pictured his charming face. It was
better than nothing.

The next day began a steady assault of romance and
courtship that would have shamed the most avid Don
Juan. For over a week Kate found herself the recipient of candy, tiny notes filled with poems and whimsical sayings, a singing telegram proclaiming true love,
bottles of champagne and baskets of cookies.

Liz was remarkably restrained throughout most of
the week, limiting herself to a few sly grins and stifled
laughs. Kate didn't know how to react. She wondered
if he was mocking her or just trying to show how much
he cared.

She never actually saw him or talked to him. In fact
he was suspiciously absent from his office. Even Liz
had remarked that his secretary said he had cut way

back on his workload and disappeared for hours at a time. She didn't know where he went, but judging from the Giant's ticket stubs she found on his desk he was seeing a lot of baseball games.

The final coup came late Friday afternoon as Kate was finishing up with a client. An elegant gentleman in a black tuxedo came to the door with a silver tray and on it a pristine white envelope marked personal and confidential to Kate Marlowe.

Under the curious eyes of Liz and one of her clients, Kate read the extraordinary message. Her eyes brimmed with tears as she wordlessly handed the note to Liz who read it aloud.

Dear Kate,
I love you more than life itself. Please, will you marry me?

Love, Barrett

"Oh, how romantic," the young bride gushed. "That's beautiful."

Kate stared at Liz with a confused expression on her face, as she took the card back in her hand.

"She's right. You couldn't have asked for a more romantic proposal," Liz said dryly. "What's wrong?"

"I don't know," she replied, a troubled light in her eyes. "It's everything I hoped for and yet..." Without another word, she grabbed her purse and fled out of the office leaving Liz and her client staring after her in shock.

When she got to the street she walked aimlessly for blocks, not noticing anything at all. Her mind was whirling with unanswered questions. Why wasn't she happy? Barrett wanted to marry her. She should be ecstatic, and the way he had courted her with romance was more than she could have asked for, but something was missing.

It took her three miles to figure out what was wrong and another two miles to figure out how to fix it.

The game was already in the third inning by the time Kate got to the ballpark. She barely glanced at her ticket as she walked toward the reserved section where she knew Barrett would be sitting.

For a moment she couldn't see anything, as the fans in front of her jumped to their feet. She peered over shoulders and in between bodies trying to remember exactly where his seats were. Finally she saw him.

He was wearing a baseball cap and dressed in an old sweatshirt and jeans, and he was alone. She waited until the usher was busy and then slipped down the stairs, sliding into the seat next to him.

"Is this seat taken?" she asked as he stared at her, an unreadable expression in his dark brown eyes.

"That depends," he said. "I'm waiting for my fiancée to join me."

"Oh, well maybe I can sit here until she comes."

He stared at her and then turned back toward the field. "I don't want to play games, Kate," he said, trying to hide the pain in his voice.

"I don't, either," she replied, following his gaze out to the field where a new pitcher was warming up. "That's why I came to see you. I want you to stop sending me flowers and candy and everything else that you've been doing.''

"I thought that's what you wanted," he said grimly. "I guess the romantic remedy didn't work this time, did it?"

"Is that what this is all about? A romantic remedy?"

"No, it's about the fact that I love you," he said, turning to face her. "I want to marry you. I don't know what's going to happen with us, but I do know that I can't spend the rest of my life wondering how it might have been if I hadn't been too scared to take a chance. That's why I did all that romantic stuff. I thought maybe it would change your mind about us."

"It didn't," she said, a loving gleam in her eyes. "It didn't have to, because I love you, too. And I realized that all the romance in the world isn't worth anything if you aren't with me to share it. Those romantic remedies I toss out aren't really about romance, they're about love, about two people being together and sharing their lives. I do want to marry you, but only if you really feel that you want the same thing." Her blue eyes pleaded with him for reassurance.

"I do. I admit the idea still scares me, but deep in my heart, I know that this is right. The last few weeks have been horrible without you. I felt like the sunlight had gone out of my life. I know that I don't want to lose you, and your optimism, and your crazy, quirky, romantic ideas," he said with just a trace of laughter. "I want whatever you want."

"I feel the same way," she replied. "I just need you, not all the flowers and candy. I just want to be with you, whether it's a baseball game or anywhere else,'' she added with a wide smile.

Barrett grinned. "You mean you'll go with me to baseball games, basketball games and football games—"

"Don't push your luck," she warned, as he gathered her in his arms and kissed her with complete disregard for propriety.

A burst of applause and cheering broke them apart and Kate gazed breathlessly into his eyes as Barrett yelled out, "We're getting married."

"We know," one guy yelled back, pointing at the scoreboard.

"The answer is yes, Barrett." The flashing lights beamed throughout the park.

"I can't believe you did that," he groaned, crushing her against his chest.

"I can't believe I just got engaged in the middle of a baseball game."

"I love you, Kate. Let's get the hell out of here."

He pulled her laughingly through the crowded stadium until they were finally alone under the harsh lights of the silent parking lot. Kate didn't see the empty beer cans or the half-smoked cigarette butts. She didn't see anything but the man she loved and the man who loved her.

*   *   *   *   *

Diamond Jubilee Collection

It's our 10th Anniversary... and *you* get a present!

This collection of early Silhouette Romances features novels written by three of your favorite authors:

ANN MAJOR—*Wild Lady*
ANNETTE BROADRICK—*Circumstantial Evidence*
DIXIE BROWNING—*Island on the Hill*

* These Silhouette Romance titles were first published in the early 1980s and have not been available since!

* Beautiful Collector's Edition bound in antique green simulated leather to last a lifetime!

* Embossed in gold on the cover and spine!

✂ **PROOF OF PURCHASE**

COMING SOON...

For years Harlequin and Silhouette novels have been taking readers places—but only in their imaginations.

This fall look for PASSPORT TO ROMANCE, a promotion that could take you around the corner or around the world!

Watch for it in September!

★